WOMAN SCORNED
C. J. DARKE

Copyright © 2024 by C. J. Darke. All Rights Reserved.

No part of this publication may be reproduced, distributed, or transmitted in any form or by any means, including photocopying, recording, or other electronic or mechanical methods, without the prior written permission of the publisher, except in the case of brief quotations embodied in critical reviews and certain other noncommercial uses permitted by copyright law.

ISBN: 979-8-3249727-4-5

First Edition May 2024

Edited by Tiffany Avery
Cover design by C M Parker

This novel is a work of fiction. Names and characters are the product of the author's imagination. Any resemblance to actual persons, living or dead, is entirely coincidental.

This book is dedicated to Declan and Taylor - You are, and always will, be the centre of my universe.

Special Thanks to Claire, Karon, Jamie, Tony & DJ. When times were tough, you guys pushed me toward my dream.

I am eternally grateful.

To Tiffany - I may have written a book, but you brought it to life.

PART ONE

CHAPTER ONE

November 4, 2017

My head was on the edge of obliteration, and three more rings on that phone would trigger the almighty explosion. One brain, two faces. There was nothing I loathed more than a migraine.

"Hi, Steph."

"Hey, Mom," I returned, glancing at the clock. "Do you know what time it is? I'll tell you. It's almost midnight. Why are you even up this late? Could you call back when the brightness of the Texas sun has reared its not-so-beautiful face? Please, Mom. Now's not—"

"Forgive me for worrying about my only daughter," she interrupted. "It's Ricardo. I don't trust him, even if he is a detective. When will you find yourself a real man who'll love you for who you are? Oh, and where's he supposed to be this time?"

"If you're talking about my boyfriend, he's on another of those stakeouts, possibly in Austin. He can't discuss the case until it's solved, but he'll be home soon. Please don't make my head hurt more than it already does. We're not doing this tonight."

"But Steph."

"But nothing, Mom," I said, my hand resting against my forehead. "I feel like crap. I can't do this right now."

"Then when can you do it? You should come home and be with the ones you love the most. We'll care for you, and our beautiful granddaughter will want for nothing."

I closed my eyes to the pounding pain. "How many times can we do this before enough is enough?" I asked. "It's every day. Ricardo's a good guy, and you should give him a chance. Yes, he works long hours, but it comes with the job. I don't want to fall out with you, so quit with the crucifixion. It gets tedious after it's preached a thousand times."

"Your naiveté sees something different from any other, and he's played you for over a year. Ricardo can't love anybody but himself. You'll eventually get hurt."

"He called to tell me how they'd finished for the night," I told her, fleetingly pushing the phone away from my ear. "Ricardo's considerate. He'll have left Austin and should be home soon."

Mom paused, but she rarely let things go so quickly.

"Then tell me why Randy Newman says otherwise? The one you claim to love is drunk at the bar again. How many times, Steph? It's three, and that's only this week. He's been there since eleven this morning, and the only thing he stakes out are those pretty young girls when he drops another bill into their panty line. When will you listen? All he does is lie to you."

"Please don't call me Steph. You know how I hate it when you call me that. Anyway, he probably celebrates a win as another bad guy is slammed behind the steel. Ricardo treats me well, so how about you drop the assassination? Please, Mom. I'm happy. He doesn't hit me like Pete once did. Spend time with him. You'll see how loving he can be."

"If something doesn't smell right, it's probably not. I don't like it, Stephanie. Don't hesitate to make that break if he causes you any hurt. I don't trust him. I never have. Not since Pops found those reports in the archives."

My eyes rolled as my brain continued to thump against the world. "And those allegations were proven to be false," I returned. "Ricardo says only cowards hit women, and I believe him. Listen, I best go. I don't feel good."

"What's wrong?" she asked.

"Those migraines have worsened since the pregnancy was confirmed, but it's worth it. I can't wait. She's everything I ever wanted, and my baby girl will be somebody to call my own. Love you. We'll speak soon."

"Pops sends his love," Mom said. "I'll call you tomorrow."

I thought about those lies I'd told her, and a thousand ants crawled the stem of my back. Ricardo had hit me before, three times to be exact. He'd often get out his aggression by smashing the bad apples from the nearby orchard with a baseball bat. There was an occasion when he didn't see me, and I took it to my face. I'm talking about the wood, not the fruit. He claimed it was an accident, and I believed him. Ricardo wouldn't be so cruel.

I nursed a broken jaw and four stitches to my lip, but accidents happen. No accident more significant than the little one in my stomach. She wasn't exactly planned, but Heidi, the name I'd picked for her, was the best thing ever.

My gaze caught the blur of the phone, and I thought about a past conversation. As much as I loved Mom, I prayed for the day she backed away from my love life. It was a weekly occurrence, and it was getting me down. Being a detective in Texas was a dangerous job, so Ricardo deserved a little alone time at the bar.

I was about to return to the sofa when the phone rang again. I wanted to throw the stupid thing against the wall, but it would cause too much pain. I was slow to answer. "Mom, will you quit with—"

"Stephanie, it's Sapphire," interrupted the female voice. "I hope you and the little bump are doing okay. You should come to the bar. Ricardo's had much to drink, and, well, you know, Mitch won't serve him anymore. Please come and collect him. It's not good for business. You there, Stephanie?"

"Sorry, Sapphire, I just can't do it. Not while my head has me incapacitated. Another time, but not tonight." My eyes pushed beyond the boundaries of my face. "You're the bar owner, and I've told you many times to get some security. There must be someone else who can give him a ride home."

"Mitch and I are the last on our feet, but the poor kid should have finished his shift an hour ago. Ricardo's supposed to uphold the law, yet those detectives do nothing but break it. They've roughed up the place, and it'll cost heaps for repairs. You need to come over. If anybody can drag his sorry ass from the counter, it's you. When Ricardo leaves, the others go, too. I could do with your help here."

"I'll try, but no promises."

My phone fell to the wooden floor, yet I didn't care if it broke. I was past caring about most things in life. "Why won't anybody let us sleep?"

CHAPTER TWO

Minutes later, I'd partially dressed, reluctantly climbed into the car, and clicked the engine into gear. I hated winter, especially at midnight and beyond, when the occasional iceberg would push against my face. I could somehow be cold amid a volcanic eruption.

Why did he make me do this so late at night? I slammed a hand against the wheel before covering my ears with my white woolly hat. I was in no condition to be out this late. I was in no condition to be anywhere except clinging to the sofa.

I stared at my cabin for one last time, gripped by the emptiness inside.

But then my hands fell to my stomach, and a bolt of warmth shot through me. "Hey, precious, that's a big kick. You'll be a soccer player, and I'll be the proud mom who watches on those lines. You'll also be the most beautiful girl in the world. But listen to me. It's time to focus in. No more kicking, not tonight. It's dark, and I have to pick up Daddy. You know how it is. I have to keep my skylights on the road."

The three million trees seemed to bend menacingly across the twists, yet they were feral tricks of an optical illusion.

Cedar Creek was beautiful, but living life on the outskirts of Caddo Lake had it beat. It was on the Texas side of the border, and the place was majestical. It was a fairytale yet to be created, even if those dark, imposing trees scared the crap out of me.

I neared the bar, and the little warrior hadn't stopped kicking for ten minutes.

That was until I killed the engine of my gray Silverado. "Hey, no going back into your shell. You'll hear Daddy soon, so how about one more kick? Okay, precious. Rest up for the night, and we'll speak more in the morning. Love you." I gently rubbed my stomach.

As I stared at the bar, the thump in my brain returned, more brutal than ever. My head was caught amid the wrap of an overpowering python.

I opened the car door and threw up last night's supper. Wow, I didn't think a small Texan girl like me could create such a mess.

But then my hands reunited with my stomach, and the world fell upon a moment's tranquility. Ricardo would be drunk, but that's when a guy lets out his emotions. He'd confess his genuine love for me, then tell the world how much he loves our baby girl, too. There had to be a first time.

I climbed out of the car and wiped my mouth on a sleeve. Screw the puke. My incredible family would soon be complete, and that's all I ever dreamed of.

I walked toward Juniper Lights, but my stride began to shrink. Another squelch. Another moment to wonder why they built the bar so near to the freaking wetlands.

Frustration turned to anger when I fell into the gunk, but I was relieved to have landed on my side. "Fuck! Fuck! Fuck! You've made me lose my hat, and there's crap in my hair! Would you have done this to me if I were a brunette? Didn't think so. Yes, because this won't be noticeable when I walk into a crowded bar. Do blondes really have more fun? Wouldn't that be a day? I call it bullcrap. Thanks a bunch, God."

I would have screamed, but I didn't want Heidi to be grouchy in the morning.

With crap on my hand and my hair covered in swamp, I moved closer to the doors. My steps were much smaller than before, which should have been impossible. Back then, they barely existed.

I headed inside, but it was quieter than I imagined. There wasn't a soul to be seen. Sapphire wasn't wrong, and the place was a mess. It usually was, but things had undoubtedly gotten heavy last night.

There were so many tables upturned, and I counted at least four stools with two legs instead of three. Even the jukebox had been smashed up.

The floor crunched at my every movement. What had he done?

I was reluctant to push on, yet my feet took me forward, but then I stopped to the muffled voices that came from behind the pool table.

Returning to my car would make me feel safe, but my conscience wouldn't allow it. I continued toward the table.

"No, get off me! Ricardo, don't you dare. I'm saying no. Hear me, asshole. I said no!"

I peered around the table to see him leaning over Sapphire. I knew it was her due to the silver buckles on her shiny, black boots. Her face was being aggressively pushed against a leather sofa, and she struggled for breath. I initially thought it was a bust, but then I noticed her torn black cami and short leather skirt. The latter had been forced over her hips.

Sapphire appeared to fight with everything she had, arms swinging, her legs kicking, but then he ripped off her black and white spotted panties. I knew his game. It hit me like a freight train.

He was trying to rape her.

As he fumbled for his buckle, I shook off the moment's trauma to drag him away. "No, dammit!" I screamed, pulling at his arms. "You're hurting her!"

Ricardo rolled off the sofa and laughed when he fell to the floor. "Would you believe me if I said it's not how it looks?" Blood leaked from the scratch marks on his cheeks.

I was livid inside yet trembled in fear. "Let's get you home," I told him. "You sleep this one off."

Sapphire covered herself up, but there was a look of disgust in her gaze. Ricardo wasn't the only one to leak blood. There were a couple of spots at the back of her thighs.

"I'll speak to Chase in the morning," she said, leaning against a table for balance. "He can't get away with—it was rape! I told him no. He tried to rape me, Stephanie. God only knows what—"

"Was it a misunderstanding?" I asked, taking hold of her trembling hands. "Sorry, I shouldn't have said that."

"Go before I do something I could never regret!" Mascara ran down her face as the tears began to fall.

I don't know how, but we returned to the motor without falling into that squelch. It was too late. My robe was fit for the trash can.

Ricardo also appeared to have sobered up a little. "I'll drive," he said, his hand demanding. "Give me the keys, bitch."

I could have slapped him repeatedly as I thought about those past few minutes. "What have you done?" I said, still traumatized by the events of the bar. "I saw what happened back there."

"Give me the freaking keys!"

"No, tonight you have shotgun."

He cracked his head twice on the dash as he fell into the car. I didn't know what to do, and everything about him was anger to the power of ten. Part of me was tempted to cut my losses and walk the fifty-seven miles to Mom's, but women like me never get that far.

There were too many freaks around, and I'd do well to see daylight again.

We were minutes past Broadway when I turned to him and smiled. It was false. It couldn't be anything different. "Can you belt up?" I asked, rolling my eyes.

"Pitching another hissy fit, huh? Go ahead, keep it coming. It'll soon be a noose around your neck."

"Please, Ricardo, just put on the damn belt. What's got into you? You're no longer the guy I once knew."

"You don't know me at all, bitch. You never have, and nobody ever will. Watch where you're going, or you'll put us in the swamp." He lit up a cigarette.

"Won't you tell me what happened back there?" I asked, vigorously shaking my head. "It looked like rape. That's what it was. You tried to rape Sapphire. She said no, but you continued regardless."

My body tensed as I immediately regretted my outburst. There were infernos in his stare. Flames, both evil and cold.

I knew how much trouble I was in.

CHAPTER THREE

After three unsuccessful attempts to strap up, Ricardo threw the belt at the window. The glass shattered, and he sat there laughing. "Holy shit, did you see that?"

"You could be jailed for what you did to her!" I threw back.

"You talking about Sapphire?" His cigarette went out, so he searched his blue suit jacket for a flame. "She's a whore, and you gotta know how to handle them. You show them who and what they are, and Ricardo de Souza should be a guy who's rejoiced. I should be looked at like God. What should the world do, Steph?"

"Rejoice Ricardo de Souza?"

"You better believe it, bitch."

"No, I can't do this anymore," I said, squinting at another twist in the road. "It was rape, damn it! I want our daughter to play with her daddy in the garden and not spend her time talking through a sheet of prison glass. It's not part of the script. And please don't smoke in front of the baby. Heidi doesn't like it."

I again shouldn't have said a goddamn word, but the guilt was overwhelming.

He grabbed my wrist, and I almost lost control at a place I called Snake Corner. It would have been quite the drop had we gone over the edge.

"You saw what took place," he laughed, pushing away the

smoke from his eyes. "She came onto me. You were there, and the dumb whore was desperate for cock."

"No, what I saw was—"

"Stop the car!" he yelled, throwing his hand on the wheel. "Stop the freaking car, Steph. Do it now, or I'll send us off the concrete."

I pulled up alongside the darkness of the winding road. "Am I so bad in bed?" I asked, turning off the engine. "Am I so ugly that you have to fuck another? Look me in the eye, Ricardo. Tell me this isn't you."

"Shut the fuck up and get out!"

"You won't silence me," I continued. "I love you, but I'll never be hushed. I carry our daughter, so you should think about Heidi. Think about what it's doing to her."

"Quiet about that freaking kid of yours! It's all you talk about. I can do without an earache. And people wonder why I fuck other women. You'll get rid of that thing. We'll find a backstreet clinic and—"

"Please don't say those things," I said, tapping my stomach. "It's our miracle, and don't you think she can hear us? Heidi's clever. She understands these things."

He kicked open the passenger door. "Out of the car!"

"Ricardo, no! Get off. You're hurting me!" He clicked off my belt and dragged me by the hair.

Moments later, I was thrown into a muddy puddle, and my face fell into my hands. "Why are you doing these things to us?" I asked, the tears continuing to fall. "I love you, Ricardo. We both do, but I beg you not to hurt our baby."

He crouched, and I was blinded by his cigarette that was driven against my eyelid. My scream pierced the Texas night as I splashed the dirty water against my face.

"Shut up!" he bawled, his fingers pinching my cheek. "Only God knows why I fucked you in the first place." His smile was as dark and sinister as it was seconds ago. He again grabbed at my hair.

"I'm sorry. No, please, Ricardo. Not again. My head will explode. I can't open my eye!"

The pain intensified as I was dragged through the brush. There wasn't a part of me that hadn't suffered, and it felt like I was a carcass to a million bugs.

But the mental torture was far worse than the physical agony. The uncertainty of what was coming haunted my mind, but I clutched my stomach, hoping to protect Heidi.

The further we went, the more menacing our surroundings became. It was so dark and cold, and the greater part of me believed I'd never see Texas shine again.

He continued to drag me by the arm, and I lost count of how many times I'd smashed my head on a chopped stump. They were everywhere, and although I tried to grab one, my hold lasted moments. He punched my fingers, but I don't think they were broken.

Maybe I'd become too numb to feel anything.

But the world softened, and life became more profound than a puddle. I was up to my neck in water, and I tried to call out, but my voice fleetingly abandoned me. Rotten eggs and sulfur? I vomited for the second time tonight.

"Please, Ricardo. Where are you? Please don't do this to us."

There was a splash, and my face was pushed into the water moments later. "Shut your goddamn mouth, whore! Keep it shut and accept the inevitable."

Bubbles of panic danced before me as I tried to push him away. He was too big and strong. I was powerless for the fight. My face remained submerged in the water, and I swallowed the swamp by the gallon.

Confusion unforgivingly crushed my brain into something much smaller than an atom. I couldn't remember my name, nor did I know where I was, but then my hand broke through the water, and I clutched at the air. I had to force myself to breathe.

He'd gone, and I now stood alone amid the darkness of a merciless night.

I gasped for relief but lost my balance and caught my ankle on a rock. Once more, my head momentarily fell beneath the water as a series of white flashes bolted through my mind.

I could no longer stand straight. I couldn't put any weight on my right ankle whatsoever. I continued to choke out water.

I was wrong. Ricardo sat on dry land with a smile wider than hell.

I couldn't stay here. Not in what felt like an arctic freeze, so I pulled myself through the shallows.

I breathed respite when I finally made it beyond the water's edge. My body collapsed to the Texas mud as every inch of my surrendering flesh shivered. If I had a gun, I'd have taken my life. Who was I kidding? I'd be taking two lives instead of one.

Time passed slowly. I sat there frozen as my concern for Heidi grew more potent with each breath. I desperately needed to know she was okay, but even the slightest movement was absent.

That changed within seconds as she gave me an almighty kick. "Baby said hello," I softly muttered, my unbroken stare fixed on the water. "Perhaps she'll be a swimmer."

Ricardo got to his feet, rage displayed amid his widened stride. The back of his hand felt like a gunshot to my cheek. "I've had enough of this bullshit!" he snapped, straddling my waist and pushing my face into the sludge. "I'm your fucking clinic tonight!"

"Get off me! No, you're hurting me again!" I was once more crying oceans.

What followed were six close-fisted punches to my stomach and three to my face. My resistance was less than futile, and any strength I may have once had was left in the water.

I gazed at my muddy robe, and the glare of a reddened moon around my groin stared back. That glow darkened. I was too traumatized to blink.

Sapphire got lucky. She'd escaped the clutches of his sadistic force, but it was different for me. It felt like a sharp stick was being pushed into my groin as he continued to shove my face against the mud. My nose leaked blood. There was so much swelling on my face, and my eye had begun to close over.

Every few seconds, he stopped to catch a breath. A further volley of punches to my stomach was always quick to follow.

The bastard smiled as he continued to penetrate me.

CHAPTER FOUR

I was much too numb to move or speak, and physical pain had been slow to abandon me.

I stared intensely at my watch as my face pressed into the mud. Almost three hours had passed since we left Juniper Lights, yet the blackness of the night had turned more ominous than ever. The smell of death hung in the air.

But ominous soon became red as the night's trauma relentlessly seeped through my robe. I again felt for my stomach, but the emptiness within was slowly ingesting me.

Hollow tears of disenchantment continued to fall as my fingers reluctantly pushed at the mud. I blinked for the first time in an age. Both eyes, but then one conceded to the swelling.

I'm sure Ricardo was gone, but I dared not look behind me. I didn't dare to do anything but breathe silently.

Ten further minutes of nothingness elapsed, but then came the voice I never wanted to hear. "Bob, it's Ricky. I need to call in that favor," Ricardo said, standing a few feet before me.

The world stopped spinning as he awaited a reply.

"Like I give a damn!" he continued. "Listen up. My career's your career, and you should remember your profit on the bank job. It netted you ten large, you fat piece of fuck. If I fall, then you drop, too."

Another silence loomed as he listened to Bob's reply.

"Like you were gonna resist," Ricardo said, pressing his phone against his ear. "It's Sapphire Steal, the owner of Juniper Lights. She goes missing, okay? Sink her in the wetlands, but not too close. Call it a hundred miles minimum. Gleason won't prosecute without a body, and I'll hear about her disappearance in the morning when I wake. Remember, Bob. No trace!"

I knew what was coming but was powerless to do anything about it.

"Wake it up!" he yelled, his boot colliding with my ribs.

"You're going to… are you going to kill us?" I returned, catching my breath.

"Get to your feet. There's a place we—"

"Where are we going?" I interrupted, unable to stop myself shaking.

He pushed a serrated blade against my throat. It was the very one he'd used when skinning deer on a hunt. "Just get to your freaking feet, and quit talking!" he added, yanking at my arm.

I tried to move, but the pain in my foot was much too great. I'd busted my ankle, and the bone had pierced the skin. "I can't do this," I said, trying desperately to pull myself away from his grasp. "Please, Ricardo. I won't say… I won't say anything. I promise to keep my—"

"You know how it ends, Steph," he interrupted. "There ain't no other way this plays out."

I briefly freed myself from his hold and fell back to the gunk. There was mud in my eye, and once more, I was blinded. "Please don't do this! Think about our baby."

Ricardo took my arm and pulled me toward the water. "Think of the baby?" he laughed, his grip on my wrist tightening. "It's what I'm doing, whore! It's pest control. It's time I got rid of the vermin. You'll never live to thank me."

He chuckled when throwing me back into the mud. I was his ragdoll.

The glow of that reddened moon returned brighter than ever, and I needed more than medical attention. I needed a gravestone and a fistful of soil. I wanted to die.

Moments later, he leaned over me, grabbed my shoulder, and struck my stomach twice. His blade immediately rendered me immobile as the feeling of cold steel slipped deep into my flesh. A third strike tore through the muscle without much effort, and it felt like my innards had been ripped from my body.

I fell to my side as the blood puddled around me.

A feigned death was the only thing that could save me, so I closed my eyes and refused to move an inch. But then Ricardo laughed as his foot pressed against my back.

The sole of his boot rolled me into the shallows, yet he allowed me to float into the distance.

It was mistake number two. Ricardo also forgot to check my pulse. Perhaps they weren't errors. Maybe he intended to leave me for the gators that would occasionally be seen in this part of the world.

I sucked in a breath as my face sunk beneath the surface of the water. I floated further and further away on my front and could only pray he wouldn't spot those mistakes.

I counted to a minute before spinning onto my back. There was no other choice. I would have drowned if I held my breath any longer. The rancid taste of blood formed a clot at the back of my throat.

I pushed through the darkness of the water, occasionally pulling at the overhanging branches to keep my direction.

But I made it. I don't know how, but my knees were now glued to the mud.

I stared west to see two bright lights fade into the darkness. Were they tailing off or getting closer? It could have been another optical illusion. Perhaps I was experiencing my journey to the other side. If I was alive, I had to somehow return to the road.

I clawed at the mud and dragged myself forward.

It was working. It took an infinity, but I was nearing the brush. The pain in my ankle was relentless as the bone occasionally seeped into the squelch.

But the sludge wasn't my biggest concern. It was the dark green smartweed that had me crying again. It would cling to my limbs and refuse to let go.

I looked up at the sky and screamed. "Why are you doing this to me?" The question was rhetorical.

I caught a break minutes later, as the smartweed had been flattened, and the tree stumps were recognizable. I was briefly overpowered by relief. More so when I realized I'd miraculously returned to the place I once parked.

Four bright lights immediately forced my eyes into a timid surrender, yet it wasn't the Silverado. The gaps between those lamps were much too wide.

A white pickup stopped a few yards up the road, and three men leaped out. Two remained in the rear of the truck with rifles ready for action.

"Look what we got here, Oscar," one said, running a hand across his musty yellow beard. His eyes were big and bulbous.

"She's fucked up, Merv," Oscar replied, pushing the mud away from my gaze. "We should take her to the city."

"Please help me." I momentarily dropped my lids to the pain.

"She ain't going to no city," Merv said, "and you should

think before you act. This'll make a change from hunting wild hogs and white-tailed deer. How about we play a game, missy? I'll be damned if you ain't played it before. I call it hide, and hide some more."

"I can't feel my baby. I'm dying, and you have to get me to a hospital." I couldn't swallow my own blood, even if I wanted to.

"Only if you win the game," he nodded, his grip on his rifle tightening. "You got a five-minute start before we come chasing. If we catch you, Hank takes that body and everything that goes with it. You ain't never getting it back."

"And if I escape?"

"We gotta deal, missy?" Merv flashed me the teeth he never had. "You can run, but you ain't hiding."

A surge of adrenaline shot my broken body, but I could finally stand. My gaze became fixed on those hunters, and it couldn't end like this.

I was again on the move.

CHAPTER FIVE

I dragged myself through the sinister shadows but soon lost all sense of direction. North, south, east, or west? I could only pray I'd be closer to help whichever way I went.

The foliage was thick, and I could barely see a foot in any direction. I lost count of how many times I tripped over the smartweed, which hugged my ankle like a mom would hug her baby girl. I teared up at the thought.

There came a disturbance in the trees up ahead… thirty feet and counting. I had no choice but to throw myself to the damp earth and cling to a large piece of lumber.

But that lumber blinked, and the power of its snapping jaws brushed against my arm. I jumped back and fell on my ass, but it came a second time, tail swishing.

I pushed away and found enough energy to climb. The tree wasn't big, but it didn't need to be. I was out of reach from the jaws of a potent predator.

The adrenaline continued to push through my body.

No sooner had one problem been solved when along came another. The barrel of Merv's rifle pointed directly at my face.

"I've found her. Here she…" He disappeared into the darkness. "Get this damn thing off me!" he yelled.

The gator whooshed its tail before pulling him into view. Merv had lost a leg, but I refused to be dessert.

I was gone again and heard four loud shots echo in the distance.

Moments later, I stumbled upon another stretch of concrete. I was on my knees when I saw four bright lights up ahead. Those lights were instantly recognizable—it was the pickup truck.

I could have screamed, but I closed my eyes to a snapping twig behind me. A kill shot was to be expected, yet there was nothing but a drawn-out hush.

That silence was soon snapped. "Don't be scared."

I turned to see Oscar place his rifle on the road, but then he backed away, palms facing me. "Ain't no need to be scared, lady," he said with fear in his eyes. "I ain't gonna hurt you." He pointed at the empty truck. "Take my hand. You gotta trust me. We trust each other. Take my hand!"

My legs scraped against the road as my crawl to the brush ended in abject failure. "Just kill me!" I begged. "I can't do this anymore. Pick up the gun and squeeze the—please finish me, damn you!"

He looked left and right, then sprinted toward me. "They'll be back any second. We gotta get you outta here. We go now, lady!"

He placed his jacket over my torn robe, and there was no choice but to trust him. Oscar raced me to the truck, and I was helped into into the passenger seat.

The engine roared, yet we appeared to be stuck in the mud. "C'mon, baby!" he said, his foot repeatedly hitting the pedal. "Sing to me."

"It's not... this won't work!" I glanced in the mirror, expecting the others to be behind us, but the road remained empty of threat. "We're screwed," I said, my lids beginning to fall.

"Take the wheel!" he yelled, pushing open the truck door. "We sleep when we're dead. Dad gum it. Take the wheel and keep hitting that pedal."

Oscar strained every sinew when pushing the truck, yet the tread remained glued to the mud. I slithered to the driver's side.

"It's coming!" he yelled. "One more push and you can move it."

I again checked the mirror and saw three men cautiously approach. They aimed the barrel of their guns toward us as the truck moved a few inches. "Get in!" I called out. "Hurry, Oscar, hurry!"

A gunshot pierced the air. Perhaps it was two, and I screamed when Oscar took a hit to his lower back. He lay motionless on the road, no sign of life. Regardless of what came next, I could never repay his courage.

My foot hit the pedal, leaving them trailing in my wake. They tried to give chase. They opened fire, and many small orange flashes pierced the night. Sharp shards of glass pounded against the back of my head.

But then I thought about the bigger picture. "Heidi, it's time to wake up. Please wake up, precious. Kick me. Kick me hard. I need to know you're okay."

There was no movement, not even a cramp.

"Wake up, princess. Daddy isn't here. He can't—please talk to me. Tell me you're okay. Faster, damn you! You need to go faster!" I slammed my hand against the wheel, and eighty miles per hour never felt so slow.

More lights were up ahead, and each grew brighter by the yard. Two cars played chase, but I somehow swerved between both, missing them by a finger's width.

But then the fuel light flashed red. "No, you can't do this to me!" I said, smacking the dash in frustration. "Please, no!" I dropped my head onto the wheel as the truck began to slow. I should have let the swamp take me. It did take me. Everything I'd encountered played a role in my impending demise.

Join me, Mommy. I don't want to be alone.

I let go of the wheel as the vehicle rolled left.

Black on black. Sleep to sleep. My head spun, and I conceded to the silence of the surrounding wetlands.

CHAPTER SIX

December 17, 2017

I opened my eyes, but they immediately closed to the blinding shine. It felt like my entire body had fallen through the soft, white clouds of heaven before tripping into the fiery depths of hell.

The stench of a swamp. That deceptive lumber. The way Ricardo repeatedly pushed his cold steel into the shell of my gut. Those flashbacks were harrowing. Each was a haunting image that would remain with me forever.

He left me to die. Ricardo was responsible for everything that happened last night and I remained trapped between the darkened clouds of loss and the raging infernos of eternal anger.

The thought alone had me destroyed.

I forcefully pushed open my eyes to see a white blur zipping about the room. "It had to be a dream," I said, gripping the bed sheets. "Please tell me last night was a nightmare. Tell me Heidi's okay."

"I'm Dr. Breech. It's good to see you've finally rejoined the land of the living. We almost lost you. Technically, we did lose you twice, yet your refusal to touch the light was beyond admirable."

I remained silent to his English accent. The blur faded.

He placed his chart on the bed before undoing the top button of his crystal blue shirt. "And along comes the inevitable dumb question," he said, wagging his finger. "How are you feeling?"

I gazed into his deep blue eyes before trailing to his smile of discomfort. There were so many questions, yet one stood out. I already knew the answer, and my guts were suddenly ripped from my stomach.

"Am I here because of the migraine?" I asked an entirely different question. "I need answers. I feel drugged. There's so much confusion."

"It's too early for questions," he replied, perching at the foot of the bed. "You should—"

"I need to know what happened last night. I need answers."

"You've been here for six weeks, give or take, and most has been spent drifting in and out of consciousness. Like it or not, the drugs were the only way to keep you alive. I've changed them to a lower dosage, and although you remain undeniably weak, you heal well."

A tremor of pain shot through my foot as I tried hard to recall past events. Things remained distorted. "What happened to me?"

"You were in bad shape when they brought you in, but we'll go no further. Not until you can deal with those answers."

"I'm strong. Do I need to ask again? What happened to me, doctor?"

"You had three surgeries in total. The dislocation of your ankle was made worse by the compound fracture to the tibia, and you'll wear a boot for another few weeks."

I slowly sat up, back straight. "And Heidi? I lost her, didn't I?"

"The damage to your stomach was what almost took your life. I've seen nothing like it, at least not from somebody who survived. You also had four dislocated fingers and many lacerations, although most of the latter were superficial."

"I can't stay. I have to see Mom."

"And she can visit tomorrow. Your body needs to heal, and I suggest you remain at Greenfields Hospital for a further week. Please don't fight me on this."

My hand came to rest on my ribs but would go no further. "You keep swerving the question. Did I or did I not lose my baby?"

He closed his eyes and pushed out a deliberate breath. "It's a shock. I couldn't imagine it to be anything else, but—"

"I need to be alone."

He remained uncomfortable while standing to the left of the bed. "Two or three detectives are hanging around," he said, pointing toward the door. "They occasionally drop by and have done so since you were admitted. It's your call. I could ask them to return in the morning."

"Send them in. They need to know what Ricardo did to us."

"Okay, and I'll have somebody ready the transport after they're done."

"Am I being discharged?" I threw back, confused by a previous statement.

Dr. Breech pointed at the wheelchair in the west corner of the room. "Not quite, although a close guided tour will help raise those spirits."

I fought back the tears as his fingers combed his thick gray beard. "Why couldn't you save her?"

"It's hard," he nodded. "I couldn't imagine how tough this is for you, and although the physical wounds will heal, psychological scars could remain forever. I'd like to refer you to a dear friend. Dr. Charles Butcher is the best in his field, and he'll help you overcome the challenges ahead."

My entire body shuddered when I stared toward the door. "Why is he here? It's Ricardo. He murdered my baby!" I repeatedly smacked the back of my head against the wall.

Breech pinned me to the bed before hitting a square red button. "Please calm down, Ms. Black. You're making no sense. Nurse Grabfast! I'll need help with—who tried to kill you?"

The nurse rushed into the room, uncertain of what was happening.

"It's him," I said. "It's Ricardo! Please don't let him in. He's here to finish me off!"

"Nurse, would you watch over the patient while I attend to more pressing matters?" Breech asked.

She smiled uncomfortably as he vacated the room.

CHAPTER SEVEN

My thoughts went into overdrive as I recalled the events of that swamp. It was my fault. Heidi would still be alive if it weren't for my goddamn ineptitude.

My heart slammed against the hollowness within. I should have said no to Sapphire.

I peered through the small glass pane, and Breech appeared to be involved in a heated exchange with Ricardo and Mallory. The same Detective Bob Mallory who had the task of silencing Sapphire.

I prayed to God that he failed. I could no longer pray. God no longer existed. He didn't to me.

The doctor returned to the room, and although Ricardo wasn't with him, Mallory was. "I'm sorry, Ms. Black," Breech said, his eyes apologetic. "I don't have much leverage by way of law enforcement, but security will keep Ricardo away. Detective Mallory would like to know more about what occurred in November."

Would I die here, or was my pulse fated to be taken between the four wooden walls of my castle? The rancid stench of decomposition fleetingly danced in the air.

Breech stared him in the eye, and a brigand of feral flames were desperate to be let loose from the asphyxiation surrounding them. The doctor didn't like being undermined, but he soon left the room.

As Mallory sat beside me, his grin grew wider than a

canyon. "Alone at last, huh?" he said, casually eyeing me up and down. "You look different than the last time I saw you. There's less swelling. You got more color to those soft, beautiful cheeks."

His hand felt for my face, but I pushed it away. "Leave me alone."

"How about we move this along?" he chuckled, glancing at his watch. "You know how it is. Dollars to make and whores to be fucked."

"Please... please leave." It felt like I'd swallowed Arizona.

"It's good news," he continued. "We have the guy responsible, and he'll wait for his judgment. Those damn negroes get everywhere."

"I need a real cop, so why don't you quit with the racism and find me one," I replied. "You know who did this, yet you're another damn cog in his machine."

He pushed his brown leather jacket to the side, revealing one helluva smoker. "Only a crazy dances next to the gloom of an unfortunate gravestone," he chuckled. "It was one of those coons, and that's what it'll say in your statement. Lady Luck's given you another chance, but it don't happen twice. That goddamn bitch is incapacitated."

Part of me expected to be slugged where I lay, so I tried not to make eye contact with him. I couldn't see the bullet that would end me.

"That's not what happened!" I eventually returned.

He began to remove the bandage from my head. "It was dark," Mallory nodded. "You didn't see anybody except another damn negro. How could you forget the color of his skin and the ink beneath the eye? Remember the eye. Four teardrops below the left socket, all created by ink. Wow, Ricardo never held back." He stared at the stitching.

"You have this wrong."

"How can I be anything other than impressed? Could such a delicate skull receive a second mauling?"

"You're asking me to put an innocent man on—no, I won't do it. You're mistaken if you think I'll be his executioner. Ricardo was responsible, and you took care of Sapphire. Tell me I'm wrong."

He pushed his jacket back into place before fixing the dressing. "Get off me!" I added.

"Chicane O'Neil wouldn't know innocence if it bit him on his ass. What about the sisters he gutted near Lodi? Triplets, and fifteen years young. We didn't have enough on him, but this time is different. That murdering sonofabitch will get what's coming. Remember the ink and the color of his skin. Do we sing the same song?"

"Where did you bury her? I was there. I heard the intentions."

He slammed a hand against the bed. "Shut the fuck up about Sapphire! I'm sick of hearing the name."

"You make me want to puke," I said. "You're even beginning to sound like Ricardo!"

The door opened, and into the room stepped another suit. I may have seen her this morning, but things were a blur back then.

There was something authoritative about her. Something compelling, and she didn't take her eyes off Mallory, not even for a moment. Whatever she took, I wanted some by the bucket.

Three cops followed her, but it wasn't solely the room that had become busy. The corridor had, too.

Those guys were everywhere.

CHAPTER EIGHT

She flashed her badge as her stride took her toward her intended target. "Lieutenant Gemini Shultz, Internal Affairs." The cop swiped Mallory's gun from his waist before he could blink. "I offered you the rope, and you tripped to the gallows. Somebody's in a whole lot of trouble."

Mallory took a step back as his jaw dropped to the floor. "Hey, what's the freaking deal?" he asked, his arms outstretched.

"Detective Bob Mallory. I'm arresting you for deception, conspiracy to murder, and the disappearance of Sapphire Steal. We'll say hello to Miranda when we return to the—"

"I don't understand?" he said.

She reached beneath the bed and pulled out what appeared to be a recording device. It flashed red every few seconds. "Where's de Souza?" she asked, her eyes slight and her tone demanding.

Mallory fell silent.

"Answer me, asshole," Shultz added. "You shouldn't be blinded by loyalty, nor should you piss on a woman going through menopause. You're facing the full force of Internal Affairs, and I'll throw away that key."

His face fell into his hands. "This can't be happening. I've done nothing wrong."

"And you can tell it to the jury." She gave him a devilish

smile while snatching his badge off his jacket. "I'll take this, too. It's no longer needed. Cuff him, boys. Make them nice and tight. Mallory chose to swim in a puddle of corruption, so he should know how deep it's become. Do we have any sightings of de Souza?"

"Nothing yet, Lieutenant," one of her colleagues said. "The bottom two floors have been checked and cleared."

"Every room must be searched," Shultz returned. "If it's dark, you don't stop looking until it's light. He has to be somewhere around here."

Mallory's head was pushed forward as his murdering hands were pinned behind his back. Out came the silver bracelets.

"You got this wrong," the detective muttered, struggling to break his restraints. "Ease the fuck off!"

I waved him goodbye.

"Take him to the car," the lieutenant said, slowly moving toward the exit. "I want two cops watching his front and the same at his rear. There's to be no repeat of last week's events, and this sonofabitch doesn't break free. He's down for a ride. Only then will he face his true day of reckoning."

My surroundings began to empty, but a male nurse had snuck beneath the radar. He loitered at the room's far side so he was easily missed. "Easily missed?" It was a statement made in haste. He was undeniably handsome, and his face wouldn't be lost in a crowded bar.

I think his eyes were hazel green, although I couldn't be sure as the room had fallen to a deadly shade of sallow.

He was a woman's warm dream turned hot.

"Hi, Ms. Black," he said, struggling to look me in the eye. "You won't know me, but I'm, umm… I'm Nurse Trapp."

I stared at his black, wavy hair and shrugged. "Is there a

reason why you're here?" I was playing it cool.

He went to rest his hands on the chair but missed, and I instantly felt his embarrassment. One of us had to remain calm, even if my heart beat furiously.

"Well, it's James, but most call me... everybody calls me Mouse," he added. "It's stupid, I know, but it is what... yeah. Good to see you've joined the land of the—"

"Living?" I uncomfortably smiled, feeling a cramp in my side. "I've been there and done it. Would you believe me if I told you I'd become the sole owner of the closet?"

I momentarily closed my eyes, but he disappeared when I opened them again. "Hey, where did you go?" I asked, staring at the dull, ivory walls.

"Down here." I turned to his voice to see him partially hidden beneath a crisp, white bed sheet. His long, thin finger pressed against his lips. "Shh, keep it down."

"Like this isn't strange enough already," I said, my hand hovering over a big red button. "I fail to understand why a nurse is on his hands and knees at the side of my bed. Have I unknowingly strayed onto the set of an impending porn flick? I want answers, Mouse. Don't make me hit this bell."

He shook his head, eyes pleading. "I'm screwed if Breech catches me here again. He's already warned me to stay clear, and this is my last... shit, he's coming."

The door opened, and the doctor stepped into the room. "Is everything okay?" he asked, checking behind the door. "I could have sworn there was another voice. It sounded like Mouse; I mean James."

I stuck out my hands and pretended to be cuffed. "You got me, officer. I was talking to myself. I'm trying to strengthen my throat, and you know how it is. Oh, and I've seen no mouse. Is there something you're not telling me? I've dealt with enough rodent infestations to have lasted a lifetime. Sorry, I'm talking about my bad choice of boyfriends."

James raised his thumbs and smiled.

But my stomach flipped when I remembered Ricardo. "Did they get him?" I asked, dropping my hands to the bed. "Tell me he's on his way to the precinct."

"If you're talking about Ricardo, then don't worry. He stole a nurse's uniform and escaped via the back door, but he'd be stupid to return."

"You don't know him as well as I do," I replied. "He'll be itching for revenge."

"Have you bumped into Nurse Trapp yet?" Breech swiftly changed the subject. "Although James is new to the game and eager to impress, I've asked him to remain distant. The boy likes to help, but he can try too hard. That said, he was an asset when you came in that night. You were his first emergency."

"An asset?"

"James doesn't often work in that department, but we were short of staff. He has enormous potential."

"I'm sure he's harmless, but I won't hesitate to kick his nutsack if he causes trouble. I will when they remove the damn boot." I giggled when I saw James suck in his cheeks and cover his groin.

Breech nodded while staring at the chart. "That boy spent every break reading at your bedside, and he believed you'd pull through. He also heard you talk about de Souza as you slept last night."

"Talk about him?"

"You've suffered many nightmares since you were admitted, so it was another bad dream. His father was once a DA, and James pulled a few strings. Internal Affairs took care of what followed. You should rest. Too much excitement in a day will be a step back in your quest for rehabilitation. I spoke to your mom earlier, and she'll visit in the morning. I must go."

The door gently closed, and the meerkat came up for air. "That was stupidly close," he laughed, getting to his feet and wiping his brow. "He'd have my balls in a slingshot if he found me here again. Thank you. Thank you. Thank you. Did I say thank you?"

"You're weird," I told him, rubbing my eyes. "I don't think I've ever had such a strange and surreal encounter. Okay, maybe there was one."

He moved toward the exit but turned to me and smiled. "Ricardo is a moron," James said. "He has it coming, and I hope the guy shakes hands with the executioner before his head falls off. Rant over. I'm sorry to, you know, disturb you. I heard you were awake and had to visit. And the creepiest award of the year goes to… I'm sorry."

He was gone moments later.

James made me smile, and there hadn't been many times when I'd done such a thing. I closed my eyes, and my pulse finally returned to normality.

Things changed moments later, and I was swarmed by sadness when recalling the night at the swamp. Ricardo deserved capital punishment for what he'd done to Sapphire, and I'd have loved nothing more than to hit the goddamn switch myself.

But warmth soon became the overpowering force as I imagined how cute James looked when he peered over the bed sheets. The relief in his gaze and that childlike smile. He was a whacko, yet I felt an immediate affinity for him.

He's nice, Mommy.

It sounded wild, yet I was sure I'd met my guardian angel.

CHAPTER NINE

Hours passed, but there was zero chance of me catching any crash. Not while Ricardo remained at the front of my mind. Sometimes, I'd stare toward the door, and my sweats would run hot.

You'll soon be okay, Mommy.

The darkness of that swamp, a lump of lumber, and the frost of a blade that tore through my flesh. Each was an image that chilled me to the bone. I wondered if I'd last long enough to return to my cabin.

Why did he do those things? It was a question I'd repeatedly asked myself, yet only one person knew the answer. He remained on the run.

My hands grabbed at the sheets as I heard a creak by the door, but much to my relief, James popped his head into the room. I was able to breathe easier.

"You awake, Ms. Black?" he asked, almost waiting for permission to enter.

"Would you be stalking me if I said no?"

"I'd wonder if you were sleep-talking again. Sorry, but I'm on a break, and I was wondering if you wanted to go for a spin."

"Why don't you come on in?" I said, my head dropping back to the pillow. "You shouldn't get into trouble with Breech."

The door closed, and he quietly moved toward the wheelchair. "Edward's done for the night, so you're stuck with me. Three work the shift, but the others don't share the same captivation as yours truly. You won't know them. It's their first time here."

To keep him grounded, I'd have loved nothing more than to tell him he was ugly, out of shape, and repulsion personified, but who was I to dent his ego?

"Your definition of wheels slightly differs from mine," I smiled. "Sorry, Mouse, I can't watch you struggle anymore. Mom had one of those chairs after her hip replacement. The green button opens the armrests."

"The green button?" he nodded. "Yeah, I knew that. Anyway, who's taking whom for a ride? It may not be turbocharged, nor would it pass for the Indy, but this smokes whenever James Trapp is on the track. Can you handle life in the fast lane?"

"Is this a good idea?"

"I'm sorry," he winced, shaking his head. "I shouldn't be here. I'll pop by in the morning, but only if you're well enough for visitors. My shift will be over, so I'll be here as a punchbag or a friend. It's your choice. You don't have to answer immediately, but I'll need to know in the next few seconds."

My heart skipped crazy beats whenever I stared into those mysterious green eyes. His presence was needed, if not addictive. "You should stay," I told him. "I could do with the company, so the question remains. Whatever does my chauffeur have in mind?"

He scratched his chiseled jaw as if to search for an answer.

"Think you can put some weight on that boot? I'd lose my job if I put you into the cockpit of speed without help. Besides, it could be—"

"Detrimental to my rehab? It's another to add to the closet." I pushed away the bed sheets and sucked in a painful breath.

I was a pencil that clung onto the rail for fear of falling off the edge.

"Care to tighten your robe?" James muttered, fleetingly closing his eyes. "I can see your... you know, your, umm... yeah, those things."

Life would have been far less embarrassing if I hadn't been born. James was eighteen, nineteen tops, and he was too young and innocent to see my breasts. Wearing blue plastic panties was the best decision ever.

The lack of a swamp was a bonus.

After seconds of trying, James finally figured out how to turn on the imaginary ignition and got down to his haunches. "Is Ms. Black ready to break the speed of sound?" he asked, his hand moving toward his ear. "Lean forward and take my grip. You grab my left. You got to trust me, okay?"

I remembered Oscar saying something similar. Merv's karma would one day arrive, and I'd smile when it happened.

"Ready to roll, Ms. Black?" he added.

"It's Stephanie," I replied, rolling my eyes. "Please don't call me by any other name."

"Loud and clear, captain." He saluted me as if I was the leader of a successful battalion.

"Wow, a man who doesn't listen. Who'd have thought?"

This was crazy—insane enough to shoot a bolt of heat through my chest. I'd felt more warmth in the last five minutes than throughout my entire life. He was my jester of the court.

I reached for his right hand; it caught him off guard, and I unintentionally fell into his arms. "I so didn't mean that," I giggled.

"This is, umm, yeah, embarrassing," he said, holding me

tightly against his chest.

There came a second bolt. Another moment of sheer and utter weirdness.

His hands were huge, soft, and trembled to the touch. He liked mine, too. James hadn't let go for an entire nine seconds. I hadn't felt so alive since I found out I was…

"Stephanie?"

"Yes, sorry, I was in another world."

"Can you go for my expectant hand this time?" he laughed, pointing to his left. "I get it. You were testing my reactions. Anyway, wrap your hand around my left bicep, but be quick. It's doing my back no good. You'll have me lying on the bed beside you."

"Why don't we put them together?" I gently placed a hand on his arm. "You can talk to me a little more. You can tell me why you make me laugh so much."

His cheeks flushed red. "Our first date, and you already have us sharing a bed? Could you be any less forward? I mean, whatever would momma say?"

I playfully smacked his hand and giggled like a nervous schoolgirl. "Your job is to satisfy my thirst for humor, not my hunger for… take that mind from the gutter. Are you leading this expedition or what?"

"Who puts a bed in such a ridiculous position?"

I again stared into his eyes, needing to know if this was just an illusion. People like James didn't exist. They didn't in my world.

"And you're sure you can steer this thing?" I asked.

"Hey, I only hit the bed twice. If I were a superhero, I'd be Colonel Hypersonic. I could give Mario a race for the bounty."

"It may have been twice, but we were yet to move. How about we blame the bed?" Things were so easy, and waterfalls began to form behind my eyes.

James passed me a red and black checkered blanket. "Here, put this over you," he said, again the gentleman. "It'll blast away any potential chill."

"Only if you take me away from this place. I'd take Lapland."

"A trip to Santa's Grotto, you mean?"

"Christmas is alien to me," I returned, a tinge of sadness in my voice. "I don't know why my folks never celebrated it, but I never saw those reindeer."

"We appear to be light on rocket fuel, so I suggest we stick to the confinements of the hospital. Stephanie, why do I sense a lack of energy about you?"

"Whatever do you mean?"

"I don't mean physically. You were once spiritual, but you somehow lost your mojo. You lack self-confidence, and I don't know why. You're the most sensational… you'll like where we're going."

James flicked the light switch, and his mischievous gaze fell beneath the glow. I realized how deep and gorgeous those eyes truly were. He was heroin, and I was a junkie in desperate need of a permanent fix.

It wasn't solely about looks. I was a sucker for charisma, and he had it in abundance. James treated me differently, too. He was gentle, warm, and understanding. Guys like him did exist, after all.

The tears began to fall.

CHAPTER TEN

James took my fingers, and his thumb soon began to massage the back of my hand. "Is everything okay or are you crying because you're happy to be around the most amazing guy in the world?" he asked.

I dabbed my cheeks with a tissue. "It's my eyes. They need to attune to the brightness of the world again."

"I believe you, but millions wouldn't," he said, flashing a caring smile. "Everything's okay. It's going to be fine."

Would he ever stop ticking boxes?

"Where are we going?" I asked. He could have led me into the eye of a storm, and it wouldn't have mattered. James understood me, and we'd made one helluva connection. "Not going to answer, huh?"

"It's a surprise," he said, springing to his feet.

Moments later, we were in the corridor, and things were quiet and dreamlike. If only Heidi had been given the same second chance.

No, I couldn't fall back into the chasm—not in front of James.

We approached an elevator minutes later, and my grip on the rest loosened. "Am I allowed to guess where you're taking me?" I asked, raising my hand. "I like games, even if I suck at them. Here's the deal. You have to tell me if I get it right."

"I presume a wrong answer results in a forfeit?" he replied.

"It's a prize, not a forfeit. Depending on your age, it could be a diaper or slippers. The clock's ticking."

"Twenty-two," he laughed, "although people think I'm younger. It's no bad thing. If they added another ten years, I'd be tagged Pappa Rat. I'll be twenty-three next month."

I exhaled an almighty breath as my face became a deadly shade of hot. "Almost twenty-three?" I said, questioning his answer. "I had you down as being a little younger."

"And the prize?"

James didn't appear to like talking about his age. I don't know. Maybe he thought I'd be freaked out and run a thousand miles because of the difference in years. He couldn't have been further from the truth.

"Okay, if I'm wrong, it's dinner at my place," I eventually returned after giving it almost no thought whatsoever. "I'll cook, but we keep things real. It's a meal between friends, nothing more."

"Your place, huh?"

His smile was so damn dreamy, but best of all… it was legal.

"We respect the boundaries," I told him. "It's two friends eating, sipping a glass of red, and sharing good company. I could use a night like that. I should also take a moment to thank you, Mouse. I'd go insane if I were alone through this. You're a special guy."

"I presume there's another forfeit if you nail it, right?"

"Then it's dinner at mine," I shot back, covering my legs with the blanket. "You get the honor of cooking and choosing the wine, but you must make me laugh. There's no deal without laughter. Can you smell that?"

"Freshly picked roses?" he replied. "I'll promise you a field of them when you leave this place. Oh, and I guess it's dinner, regardless."

James flashed me another of those soul-swiping smiles, and my innards were melting. "Sorry, I drifted. Where were we?"

He squeaked twice before wheeling me into the carriage. "If I have to reveal all, there won't be any dinner dates." He gave me a drum roll. "You should answer anyway, as a hush is the worst possible result."

"It's warm indoors, so giving me a blanket would make little sense," I snickered. "This, to me, makes it the process of elimination. Hmm, the roof or the ground? It's fifty-fifty. Okay, we're going to the ground before you whisk me away to a faraway land. Am I right?"

He hit the number nineteen button with his thumb. "Yeah, you're right," he chuckled. "You really are lame at guessing games. I'll show you something, but I'll need your trust again. It's on the roof, but this will blow your mind to the next century."

James had a gift. I don't know how, but he knew what to say or do whenever I'd be attacked by another rush of emotion. All Ricardo and Pete did was get angry, which usually led to me being tied up and humiliated. The latter often did it in front of his friends, and I'd be whipped until I bled.

We approached our destination, yet it appeared our night had drawn to a close.

NO ADMITTANCE BEYOND THIS POINT.

"Won't you get into trouble for this?" I asked, staring at the large white door.

"We give those rules the middle-finger salute. We do tonight, and I know what you need. I'll show it to you, but you have to cover your eyes."

"And I've never heard that one before," I smiled, partially shielding my face with the blanket. "Like this?"

"Your eyes, not your nose. Any cheating and I'll call you Ms. Black."

"You wouldn't dare," I said, staring at the buttons. "Won't those nurses be expecting you? You shouldn't get into—"

"I'm six minutes late from break, which means you already owe. Keep those eyes covered."

A bitter breeze took an unforgiving grip on my hands, yet I felt full of life. It only took thirty-eight years to have such feelings. "Am I good to remove this thing?" I asked. "I can barely breathe."

We went east. I'm sure it was east, although there was a little bit of north, too. Oh, and I think we traveled west before heading south. I didn't know where we were.

"Almost there," James said.

He hit the brakes moments later, and my neck conceded to the warmth of his shallow breath.

I pushed away the blanket, and tears welled up again as a thousand stars danced amid the shine of a static moon. It was majestic, more so when I saw the volcano-red sky to the west.

I'd never seen anything so beautiful.

"It's awesome, right?" James said, squatting at my side.

I remained hushed as my head rested on his shoulder. He smelled amazing. It was undoubtedly a subtle scent of innocence.

"It's the third red sky of the year," he continued, his smile wider than ever. "I'm sure there were more, but I missed them. I often spend my break gazing at the universe, but some don't understand."

"Maybe I'm one of the few who does."

"They're blinded by life and fail to see the beauty before them. I love the tranquility of the roof. It's the perfect place to chill, but you ignore the concrete barriers. They're here to send the leapers back to their rooms. The clear-up costs would be horrific."

"Can we stay forever?" I asked, hoping he'd say yes.

"Can you hear an alarm?" He pressed a finger against his mouth.

"It's not the alarm that worries me," I shot back, staring through the gap in the concrete barrier. "Can you see those flashing reds on the street? What's going on down there?"

"I should get you inside," he nodded.

Our return to the door took seconds. "Could I see that sky once more?" I asked.

"There's always tomorrow night. Maybe it'll hang around."

"Is this a lame attempt to ask me on a second date?"

James smiled when pushing open the door. "Same time?"

"I'll check my little blue book," I winked.

It would mean little to many, but the past twenty minutes were the most meaningful of my life. If Mr. Perfect existed, I'd met him the night of my admittance.

James Trapp was the puzzle I so badly wanted to solve.

CHAPTER ELEVEN

We were met by darkness when shifting through the doors. I'd have witnessed more light if the blanket had remained glued to my face.

There came footsteps, ones that scampered into the distance. My grip on the rests tightened as my bones pushed through the flesh. "What's happening, James? What's going on up here?"

"It feels wrong. Don't ask why, but I smell death. Let's get you safe."

I stared intensely at the button to the right of the elevator, but it flashed green for what felt like an eternity. I think it was green.

"I don't like it," James whispered as he bashed at the buttons. "This damn piece of crap should move quicker than—"

"It's Ricardo. This has to be him. We're sitting ducks out in the open like this. Get me out of here, Mouse, go now!"

He spun us around, and we were back on the move. His shaking fingers clutched the handle of a nearby door. It was locked.

TESTING IN PROGRESS. KEEP OUT.

My gaze returned to the elevator. It dinged twice, and the carriage was finally on the move.

James pushed at the lock with each of his keys, but the handle wouldn't click over. "C'mon, damn you!" he said, his voice now pleading for entrance.

"There's a second lock," I yelled, staring hard at his trembling fingers. "It's huge. Try the key on the left of the bunch. Hurry, Mouse. You need to get it open!"

It worked, and we closed the door, just as the elevator arrived. The world fell to darkness as James hit the light switch.

Mechanical humming could be heard in the north corner of the room. There were many shelves, and I could just about see various mechanical gizmos occupying each of them. I wanted to tell him to lock the door, but there was a freeze in my throat.

The keyhole was inches away, and although I didn't want to look, I'd succumbed to the "car crash effect." I saw crocodile skin boots, which instantly triggered a further wave of fear throughout my body.

Did he ever wear combat pants? He did, but I'm sure they were green, not brown. Green or brown? Everything was the same goddamn color! It had to be him.

Ricardo disappeared into the elevator but returned to the corridor moments later. He technically wasn't alone. The murdering sonofabitch was dragging a corpse by the legs.

It was Detective Sticklebrooke. I recognized him earlier when Internal Affairs took down Mallory and his crooked ways. He was with Lieutenant Shultz.

Blood trickled from his ear to his neck. I gasped, and James immediately pressed a hand against my mouth. My heart no longer slammed against my chest. It was beyond the point of a detonation.

A white flash bolted through my brain. There was a second when he reached for Sticklebrooke's wrist. He'd learned from his mistake.

He looked toward the three steel doors, and I couldn't recall seeing such an egotistical yet sadistic smile. He was gone again.

I heard the clunk of a door.

Twice in total, but seconds apart.

Another door. A further two clunks. Then came three whistles, although they may have been bangs. I think they were banging whistles. Perhaps they were screams?

The harsh concoction of bleach and gun smoke almost made me puke. The latter advanced aggressively through what was once the eye of my nightmare.

James pushed his palm harder against my mouth, and I could barely breathe. I guess breath didn't matter. Not now. Not while I peered through the haze to see a second body bag for the morgue. A beautiful brunette, suited but muted. A medical consultant? Her eyes were wide. She'd taken a fatal shot to the throat.

I knew this would happen. I should have said something.

The door handle turned, and James reached for my fingers. I pushed him away and was choked by regret. "You were never meant to be part of this," I said as a tremor of sadness shot through me. "You shouldn't be here."

He chuckled nervously. "There wasn't much, umm, planned for the next fifty years anyway. Life's overrated, although that sucker will work for his kills. He'll have to go through me to get to you."

He again offered his hand, but this time, I was quick to take it. I gazed intensely into his eyes, knowing that if I were to take my last breath, there was nobody I'd rather die with.

CHAPTER TWELVE

A further two gunshots pinged through the darkness before a skin-tingling silence surrounded us. James wasn't wrong regarding smelling death. I also caught the stench of decaying flesh.

That hush was broken by the hurrying footsteps that became louder by the stride. Not once had we blinked as we continued to stare into each other's eyes.

I could do little but think about the two impending scenarios. Would it be another close shave, or was there a second band of detectives with a one-way ticket to hell?

Want and expectation were two different cookies taken from the same jar.

The handle moved again, and James sped the wheels to the room's far corner.

He stepped in front of me, but I pushed him away. If I was fated to die, I wanted to see the bullet that would take my beat. It was the opposite of what happened during Mallory's visit.

The door flung open, and much to our relief, a cop burst into the room. FBI? CIA? ATF? I had no idea. It didn't matter. James was safe, and that was the main thing. The cop hit the light switch.

"Hands behind your head, sucker!" he said, the barrel of his gun aimed in James' direction. "Fall to your knees! Do it. Do it now!"

James again courageously threw himself in front of me. "I'm a nurse, and this is my patient, so how about cutting me a little slack here?"

"To your knees, asshole! Don't make me end you."

James raised an arm to his face. "Get to fuck with that light! I can't see for shit."

Another cop ran into the room and aggressively pushed him to the green vinyl floor. "Do you ever freakin' listen?" he shouted, a second gun now pointed directly at James' face.

"Check my credentials," James said, pointing to his left pocket. "Nurse Trapp, so ease up."

Three more cops swarmed the room. All were dressed in black with triggers ready to be squeezed. Life felt incredibly surreal.

"You can't do this!" I yelled, feeling the trauma of the past few minutes.

Another guy muscled to the front of the group, yet he was different from the rest. He wore a sandy-brown jacket and a matching Stetson. Was he a Texas Ranger? Whoever it was, he was corn-fed.

"Check his credentials!" he said, flashing his badge. "I wanna know if this fuck is who he says he is."

"He's good, Captain Chase," replied one of the shooters. "His ID checks out."

"You know how it rolls, dumbass! Call it through and get it checked against the database. You fresh from the academy or something?" Chase was fuming.

My eyes momentarily closed to the dozen or so bright lights. "Mouse saved my life, so back off, asshole!" It felt incredible to say such a thing.

The captain didn't blink when circling James. "Are you related to the imbecile I spoke to before?" he asked. "Answer the question, Trapp. Are you related to that idiot who doesn't know his ass from a database?"

"I was trying to—"

"It don't answer the question, boy. I asked if you're related!"

"I underestimated the—"

"It ain't the time for a midnight stroll," Chase interrupted, shaking his head. "There's a lunatic hellbent on taking her life, and she almost paid the ultimate price due to your inability to think logically."

"Sorry," James said.

"Pull a stunt like that again, and they'll be searching your ass for my boot. That sonofabitch holds the hammer, and you offered him the final goddamn nail!"

James refused to stare the captain in the eye, and who could blame him? Chase was a badass in every sense of the word.

"I'm sorry, okay?" James said, his eyes fixed on the floor. "I didn't think."

"And that's the problem with the kids of today. You never do. Folk like you should occasionally check into the real world. You come here with your fancy schooling and a stick of candy in your ass, but you ain't got no idea how it works. Welcome to reality, dumbass!"

"Hey, ease off, okay?" I threw back. "He's a friend, and I'd appreciate it if you—"

"I'm here to keep you alive, but you ain't making it easy," Chase said. "De Souza's a cop gone rogue, and you appear to have forgotten his motivation. Don't know about you, but I ain't letting him take down the star witness in a case full of worms."

My lids began to fall. "Before I return to my room, I want to know who you are," I demanded. "I'll make a complaint. I'm not impressed with how you're dealing with this. I'm sick of this bullcrap, and I'll discharge myself in the morning."

"It's Chase. Captain Victory Chase. I'm one of the new regulators you'll see around Texas. We're similar to cops, but with a much bigger—let me be clear about something. I don't know you. I don't care to know you, but you ain't going anywhere until I figure out who can be trusted."

"You can't do this!"

"I can, and I will. Although de Souza's a popular guy, he's an incredibly small fish in a large lake of corruption. I'll send him and his following freak show to hell."

"And it was him, right?" asked James.

I nodded, so Chase continued. "That murdering sonofabitch ain't gonna stop until he's finished the game. Play ball with me, lady. Don't make me fish another corpse from a swamp because I ain't ever getting used to the stench."

James' head fell into his hands. "It won't happen again. At least not without your—"

"Damn straight, it won't! You stay away from my boot, you hear? Keep your distance from Ms. Black, too." He reached for the radio that was hooked onto his shirt. "Yeah, it's Chase. Any sign of that slippery bastard? It better be good news."

"Zero sightings, Captain. The suspect appears to have flown the nest, but we have eyes in the skies. An APB was put out minutes ago, so the stingers are also in place. All nearby exits are soon to be blocked. I repeat. All nearby exits are soon to be blocked."

"I want dogs. I want lights. I want the surrounding swamps to be lit up like a freaking moon. You don't stop searching until he's wearing those bracelets. You hearing me?"

The room fell on a hush.

"I want this place searched again, again, and again," he continued. "Ten times unless we make an arrest. There ain't gonna be any stone left unturned, and I'll bury whoever refuses to get their hands dirty. I also wanna know why three detectives abandoned their posts and took an unscheduled break. Heads will roll, but mine ain't gonna be one of them."

"Yes, Captain!"

James released an almighty sigh, and he was beating himself up. "I'm sorry, Stephanie. Taking you to the Indy was a disastrous move. I only hope you can—"

"She returns to her room," Chase interrupted. "I want four cops outside her door at all times. Lunch buckets only. They can visit the restroom, but only if there's cover. No detectives. Not until I've done a little digging. Hear me now. I'll concede the badge if there's a repeat of tonight. I expect you to do the same. Only the bravest would dare to piss me off!"

Another marksman stepped into the room. "Trapp checks out," he said, waving a document in the air. "He is who he claims to be. I have his image if you need to view it."

Chase stared at James, daggers drawn, before he pointed to the door. "Get him outta here before I nail his ass to the floor!"

"It's not his fault," I shot back, hearing the whirring rotors of a passing helicopter. "I knew Ricardo would return, so if anybody's to blame, I'll take full responsibility."

"Am I talking to myself? Get him outta here!" shouted Chase.

"Will you be okay, Stephanie?" James asked.

"I'll be fine."

James was manhandled to the door by two cops. "Okay,

ease up already," he said, his palms facing the ceiling. "I'm gone."

"Will I see you again?" I asked him.

He didn't answer, and I, for one, couldn't blame him. I was a hex to anybody I'd ever encountered, and tonight typified my existence. Ricardo and Pete were akin to choosing between Lucifer or Death himself. Evil was engraved to their souls. I was surprised it only took eighteen months for Ricardo to leave me for dead.

But then I smiled as I recalled the volcano-red sky and the stars in great numbers.

James was astonishing, and what we shared was more than just a moment. If things worked out, there was a chance of a beautiful future together.

But that future could never be soon. We were just friends. It's all we could be until Ricardo was behind bars.

CHAPTER THIRTEEN

December 23, 2017

The days passed, yet each was as slow and punishing as the previous.

There were nights when I'd wake in the swamp. Others when I wondered if life could ever be the same. I didn't want it to be the same. All I'd ever known was the sting from the buckle of a belt and the horrific periods of sexual torture that followed.

If Breech was true to his word, I'd soon be discharged.

I refused to be beaten, and that determination drove me forward. Remaining here was a drain on my soul.

Chase stepped into the room as I pressed my head against the feather-packed pillow. "I'm here to thank you for the statement," he said, his face almost apologetic. "We've got enough to issue the needle. We live in hope, huh?"

"Tell me he awaits his day before the goddamn executioner."

"Not yet, but it's coming."

I sat upright, but my head slowly fell to my knees. "He broke through the blockade, right? Ricardo could be anywhere."

"De Souza won't be back, so you ain't gotta worry. We gotta sighting in Nebraska while your wheels were found in South Dakota. I've assigned you a couple of cops, just as a precaution, and it ain't gonna be different until he's—"

"Is that necessary?"

He slipped back into his shades and hat. "Ain't up for debate. Not until we have him. A black Dodge Charger will tail you, so you ain't gotta be panicked if you see one in your rearview mirror. Good news. Your discharge papers have already been signed. You're free to leave. Believe me, Ms. Black. I'll walk the world on my bare ass if we ain't got him before New Year."

"What happened to James?" I asked. "I've not seen him around since you gave him a—"

"You should listen to the doctor. What you went through was enough to have broken your mind. I should know. I've locked away enough crazies, so I know how it—"

"What happened to him?" I dug in.

"I ain't wanting to know, but stay clear. His stupidity almost cost you your life. I gotta make tracks as I'm flying to Nebraska. We'll get him, and when we do, I'll see you in the courtroom."

I felt sure James and I were more than passing ships. Things could have been amazing, and I, at last, could have been happy. I barely knew him, but he was the only guy I ever trusted. Maybe it was better this way. Who was I kidding?

Armed with nothing more than a cane and an itchy blue gown, I left the room and headed toward the elevator.

The woe was briefly overpowering, and those harrowing images could never be forgotten.

Ricardo would one day pay for his cowardly ways.

Minutes later, I approached the exit doors and jumped to the hand on my shoulder. I was relieved to see it was Breech. "Apologies, Ms. Black. I never meant to creep up on you like that, but I'm glad to have caught you."

"Thank you," I nodded. "I'm free, and you kept your word."

He gently pushed a card into my hand. "Dr. Butcher will give you all the help that's needed. He won't charge you, either, as it's a favor from one friend to another. I took a moment to call you a taxi. The fare's covered, so... oh, Lord. What the devil is he driving?"

My eyes narrowed as I continued to stare through the glass. "Who are you talking about? I can see a hotdog van and thick smoke near the engine."

"I'll wish you good luck, Ms. Black. You'll need every last bit of it."

I slowly hobbled through the doors and was fleetingly slapped on the face by a skin-gripping gust of wind. There was a time when I would have taken shelter, yet it felt refreshing and real. My left cheek tingled.

It wasn't busy—I didn't expect it to be, but I looked to the west and saw a stunning clutch of expensive cars parked regimented behind a beautiful red Porshe. "How much do these guys get paid?" I muttered under my breath.

When I stared back at the hotdog van, my heart skipped a beat. My hands were arched on either side of my nose. "James, what are you doing here?"

"It's a surprise." He removed his floppy white hat and whipped out a bunch of roses from behind his back. "For the lady. I'm talking about the flowers, not the smoke," he uncomfortably smiled.

"But I didn't think I'd see you again."

"Breech never told you, huh? I was fired for my sins, but it's cool. I'm all in for hotdogs. Who knows? Maybe I'll flip burgers next month. Life in the fast lane, right? Can you handle the excitement? Jump in."

"I'm waiting for a cab... I think."

It took three kicks for the passenger door to open. "You have options," James said. "You could pick the rich guy with the drab personality who'll get out of bed to sit on his pan. You'll wake to the smell of eggs and freshly cooked bread, and although it'll undoubtedly be your finest breakfast, it's over. The finest couldn't be beaten. It's downhill from there."

James knew how to make me giggle. I'm sure he knew how to do everything. "Options would be plural, not singular," I said. "You'll do well to coax me away from the first."

"I'm that second option. You know, the guy who paints faces with mustard because he's bored of the shitty days thrown at him. But the little he has is part of the attraction. He's real. He's a kindred spirit. He can be the one to help you fulfill those dreams. Give him a chance but heed the warning. He's all out of mustard. Anyone for ketchup?"

"You're making it hard to resist," I said, taking the roses from his hand. "Wow, they smell beautiful. I should plant some in the garden. A little color is needed in that part of the world."

Loneliness or companionship? Both scared the crap out of me, but one thing was for sure. There was no denying how special he made me feel. James Trapp was my forbidden fruit, but could I risk taking one innocent nibble?

"A ride for Black?" I turned to the yellow cab behind me. "You'll need to be quick. I've got another fare to catch."

I was torn. Undeniably so.

CHAPTER FOURTEEN

I caught Breech's gaze through the window. He nodded, and I'd received his seal of approval.

"I'll need to move this along, lady," the cab driver said, checking his rear-view mirror. "I have places to go and fares to collect."

James knew what I was thinking. It went both ways, and it was one of the reasons why we'd formed such an immediate bond. "The ride won't be needed," he confidently said to the driver. "You may have wheels, but my baby can fly like a bird."

I fanned away the receding smoke. "Seriously, Mouse. How can I put it without hurting your feelings? Do you own this piece of crap?"

"One man's junk is another man's—"

"Treasure?" I cut in, staring at the trash can on wheels. "I'm too good at this game."

I scratched my head when I saw the balloons tied to the bumper. A black letter was scribbled on each one, and it made little sense.

D-E-S-A-E-L-E-R T-S-U-J.

James laughed as he opened the hood. "You're reading it backward," he smiled.

"Just released. How cute are you?" There were more balloons hooked up to the mirrors, and James was a dream. The most pleasant dream ever created.

As I climbed into the deathtrap, the off-white door almost fell off its hinge. "You're unique, James. Don't let anybody tell you differently."

"Hey, your crap is my supersonic," he returned with a smile. "The stars or a far and distant galaxy? It's all about choices. This baby will take us to the moon if that's where you wish to go. It's got a top speed of... wait for it..."

I began to tap on the dash. "Should I roll the drumsticks or only my eyes? I'm in suspense. Won't you answer already?"

"Thirty-three miles an hour," he announced. "If I went any faster, the wheels would fall off. Do you feel lucky, punk, and can you handle a change in the stratosphere? What say you?"

My insides were churning butter. "James, you make me laugh, and the weirdness is something I could never deny. I don't fall into a stream of frustration whenever you're at my side. May I call you James, or do I follow a trend?"

"It's cool, but you're the only one with permission. See, you even get special privileges. Aren't you the lucky one?"

Many would get a Ferrari, while others had a trusty white steed, but not me. I went above and beyond and got the hotdog van. Who needs diamonds and gold?

James sat beside me and reached for my hand. "Want to talk about it?" he asked, his gaze narrowing. "I mean about what happened at the swamp. I'm here for you, Stephanie. I won't leave until you tell me to."

"You haven't asked where we're headed."

"Yeah, I kinda know where you live," he winced, fastening his belt. "Okay, that sounded mega creepy. I checked the database at the hospital. I had to. I needed your details and address. I can't believe they were stitched into your robe. It sounds lame, right?"

"See the Dodge behind us?" I said, checking my seatbelt. "They're undercover cops. They'll be around until Ricardo gets caught, and although I don't want a tail, Chase insisted."

James glanced into the mirror and chuckled. "Think we can outrun them?"

"Hate to be the bringer of bad news, but you'd struggle to remain in the slipstream of a snail. It's impossible in this trash."

"Then they have me for the long run," he replied. "I'll need to stop at a friend's. He's near Scottsville, so we'll inhale the scenery when ridding ourselves of the tail."

"How are you going to do that?"

James gave way to an oncoming car. "All you need to do is sit back and float downstream. Do you trust me?"

"I don't know why, but yes. I trust you. How will you lose them?"

"The Gods may move in mysterious ways, Ms. Black. Sorry, that was a, umm... a slip of the tongue."

Every inch of my body was a mass inferno trapped amid a volcano. I could have erupted where I sat. I was battling sensual desires. I came out on top, too. "Won't you tell me the plan?" I asked.

He looked again in the rear-view mirror. "Quit being impatient and trust the process."

Minutes later, James pointed ahead before furiously tapping at the wheel. "Damn! We're too late. See that cattle grid in the distance? No day passes when Hank doesn't push his cows through the gate, but we've missed him. We could have beat it if this thing—"

"Didn't move like a failed rocking horse on eroded wheels?" My stomach hurt as I continued to giggle.

"But we take the positives. When one route gets blocked, another shall be formed. Plan B is now in motion. I'll leave it there. It's best if you don't ask."

"I won't fall for it. I'll be strong yet clever, and I don't... okay, what's the plan? There, I said it. You got me. I concede to your charm."

I didn't know what he was scheming, but it brought excitement in exceedingly large doses. I'd never felt so rebellious.

CHAPTER FIFTEEN

That Dodge remained closer than ever, and it was as if they expected James to pull a crazy stunt. That was a problem. It wasn't possible to pull anything in this van.

But then he smiled, and I knew his mind was working the clock. "Okay, it's a little earlier than expected," James said, "but Jethro's a sight I hoped to catch. The tail shall officially be clipped."

My eyes fleetingly surrendered to the blinding rays. "I don't know who he is, but you're always into something."

There was a highway patrol car parked at the gates of Scottsville Cemetery. James rolled up beside it as I finally opened the window. I was impressed. It only took me seven attempts.

The golden beams pushed through the thick, gray cloud as unwanted beads of sweat trickled down my face. It felt more like August than December.

"Jethro's here at the same time every day," James softly said, slipping into his sunglasses. "Anyone would think he owned the place. Anyway, are you ready for this? You don't have to answer. It was rhetorical. Wish me luck." He stopped the engine.

"Problem, son?" the officer asked, his arm resting casually on the open window.

James offered a face of sheer horror. "Don't look, but there's a car behind us. They're trying to—I think they're drunk. I've never seen anyone so erratic at the wheel. He tried to run us off the road, and then they claimed to be cops. They wouldn't show us their ID."

"Is that so?"

"There was blood everywhere," James continued. "One of them was covered in it, but we spun off. They gave chase and opened fire. Help me protect her. Daisy should never see such violence."

Although James was a prankster, I had to give him his dues. He was smart and giving me an alias reduced the chance of us getting caught. I loved his wild sense of humor.

"Slow down and take a breath," Jethro said, stepping out of the car.

"He shot at us three times," James replied as the Dodge stopped in the not-too-far distance. "It was a rifle. Call it through, but don't do this on your own."

The cop flashed us a sly old grin. "Shooting guns, huh? Ain't no man firing bullets around here without my permission. Roll up your windows, folks, and lock down those doors. I'll show them who the law is around here. Don't go moving, you hear?"

"Be careful," James said, taking off his stupid hat and winking my way.

Jethro drew his weapon as he approached the Dodge. "Both out, with your fingers touching the sky. Step out, real easy. Nobody fucks with the patrol."

James hit the pedal, and we sped off at an almost seat-gripping three miles an hour! Bonnie and Clyde had nothing to fear. Their place in history would remain infamous.

I glanced into the rear-view mirror to see Jethro arguing with the others. His gun remained drawn as he pushed them against the doors.

"What's so funny?" James asked, staring me in the eye. "C'mon, you got beans to spill."

I stared at the fleshless trees to the north. "It's nothing. Everything's almost perfect."

Minutes later, James stopped the van at the corner of Hawkins. "I've got an idea," he said, opening the rusted door.

"Those regulators, or whatever you want to call them, will be here any moment, James. We don't have time for... James? James, why are you standing on the hood of your goddamn van? What part of "let's get out of here" don't you understand?"

He tore off a chunk of the signage and placed it on a dirt track that led west. "Didn't I promise to lose those turkeys?"

"This won't work," I said, profusely shaking my head. "It's the oldest trick in the book."

"And I wrote the damn thing. Let's get out of here."

His infectious personality had me hooked, but his smile was on the way to capturing my heart. I wanted it to be the first thing I saw in the morning and the last thing I kissed at night.

Everything about him made me weak at the knees.

"You're almost running on empty," I said, staring at the gauge.

"There's a gas station around the bend. It also sells groceries and power tools."

"Power tools?" My mind again went into overdrive. "I feel awkward asking this, James, but can I loan a hundred bucks? I can pay it back at the cabin."

"Beneath the paperwork in the glove box. Take what you need. It was a leaving present from Breech."

"A what?"

"Don't stress. It's not stolen," James told me. "He said I was fired and then offered me cash. He also told me to keep silent and forget it ever happened. His security failed you that night. Many people did, including yours truly. The hospital has a frosty relationship with the media, so I understand why he's trying to cover it up."

"Is that so?" I asked.

"Most of them twist and sensationalize everything to make another dollar. Breech paid me until the end of the month, and those orders would have come from above."

I headed toward the store but stopped when I saw a biker in the distance. He wore shades and a black leather jacket, and I had him down as cool but untrusting. Was I staring at one of Ricardo's sidekicks?

I thought no more about it and entered the rundown store. I was immediately greeted by the second most repulsive man I'd ever seen. Perhaps it was a little harsh. There must have been a rational explanation for why he had dog crap for breath and rabbit puke for teeth.

"Can I help?" he asked, his cheeks smeared in oil.

I shrugged my shoulders, and my face immediately reddened. "Where do I begin?"

Things were taking shape, and tonight was fated to be more than interesting.

CHAPTER SIXTEEN

The heat surpassed unforgiving, and I had to beat back the sun with my hand. "James, meet my cabin in the woods. Cabin in the woods, this is James. Could you take the van a little closer? I'm talking to you, not the building. My legs are stiff. I can do without the trek."

"Do you even have a key to get in?"

"There's a spare hidden beneath a rock by the chopped wood," I told him. "It's to the right of the front door."

Being home was amazing, and just seeing it was something I thought I'd never do again. Warmth couldn't begin to describe how I felt inside, although that may have also been related to the company I kept.

The tail returned, and James gave me the most mischievous look imaginable. "Want me to lose them again?" he asked.

"Do you always look for trouble?"

"Trouble looks for me... honest," he batted back.

"What's the point? All we'd do is move the crap from one pile to the next. The smell eventually returns. Oh, and the tail appears to have multiplied. One Dodge becomes four. Chase is taking no chances, although I expected them to be less obvious. I sometimes wonder if he's trying to catch Ricardo or scare him away."

James quickly shook his head. "It looks like a deterrent. If de Souza's dumb enough to return, he won't hang around, but

I'll take off my hat to Chase and his men. You appear to be their priority."

"I don't need him to babysit."

"Would you like me to leave?" he shot back.

"No, it's not that. I don't want to be seen as someone who needs protection. Could you grab the groceries and that new purchase of mine while I learn how to walk again? I refuse to move slower than your supersonic trailblazer."

His eyes widened as he gazed at his surroundings. "It's so tranquil around here. I wouldn't have known its existence if you hadn't given me a steer. Been here long?"

"It was an inheritance from my grandpops. I didn't get the keys until I hit the ripe old age of eighteen. It was many, many years ago. I could die here. I probably will unless—"

"It won't happen while I'm—how long would many be?"

"You shouldn't ask a lady her age," I replied, hobbling ahead.

"I didn't think you were a… I'll shut up."

If I had the energy to turn around, I would have given him the darkest glare possible. "Won't you quit being so inquisitive?" I asked. "I'm older. It's all you need to know."

"Is this the moment I tell you I'm a sucker for a cougar?" he chuckled. "Stephanie, why are you wearing the medical gown? What happened to that robe you wore when you tripped into the swamp?"

"A freaking cougar? Hey, take that back," I laughed. "Don't make me whoop that ass of…"

He drew me into his arms and dropped one helluva smacker on my lips. James was such a good kisser.

An hour later, I'd showered and changed into my only other

robe. The boot remained awkward, but I felt human again.

I walked into the kitchen and was met by a glass of red. "And she finally returns," James said. "I'm in love with the place. It's huge. It's bigger than it looks. That basement could be a continent."

"It's also soundproof," I told him. "It's where I chopped the wood when Ricardo needed his beauty sleep." There came a rap on the front door. "Could you answer that?" I asked, reaching for the groceries. "I'm about to slice the mushrooms."

"It's Mrs. Rubles," he called out seconds later. "Should I ask her to return another time?"

"Show her through."

"She hasn't come alone," he whispered, waving her inside.

I could hear him say that time and time again.

Milo and Dash burst into the kitchen and pinned me against the stove. "Oi, you two," June said to her dogs. "Give her space to breathe. It's great to see you, neighbor. We feared the worst but prayed for the best. Bless your heart. What he did was unforgivable, but this kind of thing happens if you drink at bars so late at night."

"You shouldn't listen to gossip, Mrs. Rubles," I returned, tempted to bite my fist.

If there were two people in this world, I could choose to zap to a far and distant galaxy; it was June and Burt Rubles. They were as nosey as the night was long, and I despised loose lips. And as for their dogs, Milo and Dash. Where the hell was that zapper?

"Is there something I can help you with, June?" I added. "I'm busy for the foreseeable future."

James flashed me one of his heart-melting smiles.

"Burt and I visited you at Greenfields Hospital," she said, "but we were told you weren't up for visitors. He sends his love."

"Can we do this another time?" James asked, his thumb pointing toward the door. "Dr. Breech warned how too much excitement can be dangerous. You could pop by in a day or two, or I can bring her to visit." He took a sip of his wine.

"Nurse Trapp doesn't mean to be abrupt," I added, patting his forearm. "You know what delicate flowers these youngsters can be. He's very hands-on."

James spat out his wine. "Sorry, wrong hole!"

"June, you haven't answered the question," I told her. "Is there something I can help you with? You always struggle to look me in the eye whenever you need a favor."

"You have it all wrong. I came over to see how you're doing."

I didn't believe her. I couldn't. I'd been on the end of those favors too many times. "Is that everything?" I asked.

She ran her dainty, wrinkled fingers through her tattered gray hair. "There is something, but I'll understand if you decline. Burt and I need to leave town for a few days, and I wondered if you'd care for the dogs. We go tomorrow and return Tuesday at the latest."

"It's not a good idea," James said, eyes fixed on the floor. "Sorry, I shouldn't interfere."

"No, you're right," I added. "I'm learning to walk again and can't risk them getting beneath my…" And then I thought about Ricardo. "Let's do it, although they should stay here tonight. Milo and Dash need to get used to their surroundings. You return Tuesday?"

"There's enough canned meat in the bag by the door," she nodded, stroking their noses. "Feed them twice daily, no more.

They haven't eaten today, so these two will be hungry."

"Do they behave themselves?" I asked.

"Ignore them if they act out. They're old and seek attention. We took them to the vet, and he thinks they're suffering from arthritis. I love them too much to put them out of their misery. You'll be okay looking after them, right?"

"Tuesday at the latest," I nodded, running the peppers beneath the water. "I'll make no promises after that."

"Okay, but we'll pop by before we leave. I owe you another."

She was gone moments later.

James peered over my shoulder as I began to slice the peppers. "Having the dogs here is a bad idea," he said, looking out for me again. "You need to heal up."

"I'm a big girl. I know what I'm doing."

"Then why do you slice those peppers incorrectly?" he asked. "You should slice them in eight."

"Sorry, but selling hotdogs won't make you a master at the stove."

"Here, let me show you." He slowly pushed his hands between my arms and ribs, and my neck, once more, conceded to his breath. James took the knife from my hold. He also stole my breath from within. "You start slowly before picking up the pace. Here, like this."

His groin gently brushed against my robe, and I could have died to the touch. I think I did. It wasn't the first time James had me tingling for more. "Is something happening here?" I asked, unsure if this was the moment I'd be fated to dream about.

"I don't know," he replied, "but I feel it, too."

CHAPTER SEVENTEEN

Dinner went amazingly well, although I couldn't confess to being the greatest in the kitchen. Due to the long hours Ricardo worked, I often had to fend for myself, so a mixture of pasta and vegetables was my one specialty.

We sat on opposite ends of the table, and James' smile would penetrate my defenses whenever I looked at his face of perfection. He was the sweetest guy I'd ever known, but all good things had to end. They did in my world.

"James, we should talk," I said, unsure how to tell him without breaking his confidence. "I like you more than you could imagine, but it's too early to get into anything heavy. We should wait a while. I'm mentally broken and physically worn. Then there's Ricardo. It's too dangerous for this to be anything big."

He leaned across the table, his hand came to rest on my cheek. "It's cool," he returned. "I saw what you went through, and I'll wait as long as it takes. I'm a friend. If that's all I'll ever be, it makes me the richest guy in the world. Does it mean kissing's off the agenda?"

"No tongues. I can do without… should we open another bottle of red?" I nervously laughed, trying not to think about how badly I wanted to be a part of his world.

"I'll decline, but I can get you another. If anybody deserves a treat, it's Stephanie Black."

"Don't you have someplace to be?" I asked, taking the plates to the basin.

James began to help clear the table. "If you're talking about home, then no. It's depressing. There's only so much I can take before I fall into a hole of despair."

"Is it so bad?" I asked, enchanted by his smile.

"You get what you pay for, but what I wouldn't give to live in a place like this. There's nobody in your face. It's a purer version of paradise. The company isn't bad, either."

I was now standing before a mountain of bubbles. "And you're sure about that third glass?" I asked, uncertain what part of the mess I should tackle first.

James shook his head as he scraped the leftovers into the trash can. "Being behind the wheel when you're intoxicated isn't the smartest thing to do," he shrugged. "There's a clutch of law enforcers outside, and I'd be pushing my luck. I'd be charged with another misdemeanor."

He remained an enigma, and the suspense was killing me. "Okay, tell me what you did."

"Three counts of skipping chapters and the illegal possession of a paragraph. They tried to throw the book at me, but I got probation."

"You're so silly," I giggled, scrubbing the plates.

"Nah, I plead innocence to this day. Matty, my friend, gets a bit rowdy when he's downed too much liquor. I was seeing him home when we got hooked by the cops. I could have walked, but it didn't feel right to—"

"Some were born to be the victim," I sarcastically said. "I've never been in trouble, but this sounds like Hollywood material. Keep it coming."

"Who else would look after him?" James said. "It's what friends do. Why can you be charged with a misdemeanor, but you can't be charged for a Mrs. Demeanor?"

"Those jokes are similar to the ones Grandpops used to tell me. I could spend a lifetime with you and never get bored, but you're right about the wine. You have to drive home, and we shouldn't lose control. Is this how my life's destined to be?" I gave off an almighty sigh.

He grabbed my hands and spun me around. Our lips were now inches apart. "Things will get better," he promised as I closed my eyes to his touch. "Those wounds will heal, but you don't need to be alone through this. You have a friend. He's a special one, too. I'll never pressure you into anything. Wow, this is depressing. How about we listen to music?"

I leaned forward, and our lips smacked. Majestical was the only way to describe it.

That kiss lasted moments, yet it would take me years to recover.

I pushed back the curtain, and a dark chill instantly ran up the back of my legs. Three Dodge's had their lights on, but the fourth didn't. Something was amiss.

He took hold of my hands. "You're special," he said. "Nobody could ever say different. I knew it the second I saw you. I want to know everything about you, Stephanie, but there's no rush. We can do this at your pace. I'll be here for as long as it takes."

"Oh, there's music, but only in the bedroom," I told him, trying not to fall apart at his honesty. "Can you respect the boundaries? It won't be forever. I hope not."

He followed me to my room before perching at the foot of the bed. I briefly fell dizzy as my gaze met the soft silk sheets. My hand felt for my stomach.

"CDs?" he smiled, checking out my vast collection. "I haven't seen one of those for—"

"Let me level with you, James. You can stay, but only for a while. I need to be alone. I need to learn to live without fear.

Oh, and friends can cuddle, so hit play and get that ass over here. Quit with those puppy eyes, too."

Bright fell to dim, and life felt incredibly easy. More so when my head rested against his chest. Ricardo was far too cold to give me such warmth.

But as great as the tranquility was, I jumped when I heard his cell phone ding.

I thought there were only the two of us left in the world.

CHAPTER EIGHTEEN

There came four further dings within the space of a minute, and it was driving me insane. "Hadn't you better get that?" I asked, my arm wrapped loosely around his chest.

"I'll turn it off. It's nothing I can't deal with."

I looked up and gazed into his trusting stare. "Is there a problem?"

"Okay, it's my new manager," he said, puffing out his cheeks. "You know, the one who gives me my daily routes. She can be obsessive. Amanda can be quite the character, and it's as if she wants to know my every move."

"Ooh, tell me more," I asked. "Are there skeletons in the closet?"

"I got another job after the hospital fiasco last week. I was in an office, about to show her my resume, when she sat facing me."

"It's no big deal. Not unless she rode you into submission. She didn't... did she?"

"You wouldn't be far from the truth. Amanda crossed her legs in such a way that I could see what she wore beneath. Maybe it's what she didn't wear. I don't know. I expected questions about selling and cooking shit, but I was wrong."

I sat up, my back instantly pressed against the headboard. "And after this?"

"She asked how many lovers I'd had. I'd get it if I auditioned to be a porn star, but—"

"It sounds to me like your definition of hotdogs slightly differs from hers." I wiped away the tears. "It's so funny."

"I got the job, but then she asked if she could hire me for the night. She said I'd make for the perfect love toy. Two thousand, straight up. Can you believe that shit?"

"Can't believe you were offered so much," I laughed, smacking his knee. "Did you take her up on the offer?"

"What do you... wow, whatever do you take me for?" James appeared hot and bothered.

It was playtime, and I had to continue forth with the inquisition. "How many lovers have you had, and did you think about screwing her, even for a moment?"

"None of your—no! Not even for a second. Can we change the subject?"

The scenario festered in and about my brain, and Amanda wasn't the only one who needed to cross her legs. If only James knew what he'd done to me.

"What does she look like?" I asked, throwing him an impish grin.

"She has a great body, with legs longer than my application. Oh, and then there's her hair. It's short and blonde, you know the type. It's more pixie than a cougar, but the girl's wild. Amanda's also rich. Her account wouldn't dry if you knocked seven zeros off the end. She was a regular at the country club when I worked the counter. I think it's where she recognized me from."

"You appear to have a thing for blondes," I smiled, "but it sounds like she's interested in your other potential talents."

"Then there's the tattoo of a blue butterfly. It's on the left of her ass cheek. Her name's below it, written in italics."

"How do you know these things?"

"And you can wipe that grin off your—I haven't seen it, not in the flesh!" he protested, his hands touching the sky. "She has a picture on the wall. I tried to ignore it, but the damn thing was in my face."

My gaze narrowed as I believed there was a rival. "Why does she message you?"

"Isn't it obvious?" he asked, dropping his cell phone to the bed. "I received a text last night that stunned me to oblivion. She wants to bed me while her husband watches. I mean, is this the behavior of sanity?"

His phone beeped, and James didn't hesitate to pick it up again. "I'm beginning—oh, that's just great. She threatens to kill herself if I don't meet her tonight. Amanda's beyond psychotic. I don't know what to do."

I placed a hand on his knee and smiled once more. "You should go. You should meet up and tell her how it is. Threaten to quit unless she leaves you alone. It's simple when you think about it."

"Finding a job isn't exactly the easiest thing to do. My credits stack, and I'm down for a big job that'll pay top dollar, but this is a quick win. I'm already on my final warning at home, and I'll be thrown out if I can't make the rent. I'd be a vagrant."

I covered my mouth when yawning. "You can crash on my sofa as a last resort, but only when the threat has disappeared."

"Seriously?"

"How about we take a drive tomorrow? I don't know. Somewhere distant. Someplace where there's nobody to answer to. I'm busy in the morning, but we can do it in the afternoon and evening. Who knows what may follow?"

"How does a guy refuse the advances of his sex-starved

boss without losing his job?" he said, staring hard at his last message received. "I'm not interested in anything she has to offer, and nothing will happen. I promise. Will you be okay on your own? I can stay if you need."

Our lips met for a second time. It was short and sweet, but I was laying down a marker. "Tell her you're with another and how you need for nothing in the bedroom. She'll take the hint and quit with the fixation."

James took my hand and kissed each of my fingers. "Yeah, a drive sounds magical," he excitedly said. "I'm down for a shift in the morning, but I'll swing by in the afternoon."

He reluctantly left the cabin behind.

Minutes later, I'd finished making myself a mug of hot milk, and my mind went into overdrive. There was a shadow beyond the window, and although it was blacker than the night, it was never as dark as my name.

I should have been scared, but I wasn't. Ricardo couldn't kill me twice.

Dash took shelter behind the laundry basket as Milo whimpered at my feet. "I saw it, too," I whispered. "I'm sorry. I forgot to feed you, so how about some pork, beef or chicken? Maybe you could taste some real flesh? Give me another hour, and I'll give you double helpings. Yes? No? Why am I talking to canines? See, you have me losing my mind."

I was about to hobble back to my bedroom when a horrible stench almost overpowered me. Sulfur and rotten eggs? It took all of a second to recognize that reek.

The cabin fell into complete darkness.

CHAPTER NINETEEN

I was swift to reach the closet. Arguably quicker to step inside and close the white teak doors behind me.

The lock got stuck, but all it needed was some gentle persuasion. My concealments were three winter coats, a tent, and a fleeting smell of dampness.

But then my mind returned me to the swamp, and a shiver of disgust climbed the stem of my back.

I expected his presence, it was undoubtedly destiny, although I didn't think those regulators would make it so easy. Perhaps they were on his books. Probably not. Incompetence in Texas appeared to spread like a plague.

Maybe I was doing them a disservice, Ricardo was smart, and that murdering sonofabitch was astute in most things he did. Nobody had the intellect to stop him. Nobody, except me.

There came footsteps, and each inch of my skin prickled with fear. It was moments ago when I was calm, yet things undeniably changed.

What was once distant became louder, and my trembling body was a vessel for sweat. My heart beat ferociously, and I was too afraid to breathe.

Another creak. A further skipped beat.

My gaze penetrated the gap between the doors, and Ricardo was two steps away from the bed. I saw the shadow of his arm, the silhouette of a gun gripped tightly in his hand. I must have been special, as there was a silencer attached. What had he done with his crisp blue jacket? He never went anywhere without it.

He seemed reluctant to squeeze the trigger, but it couldn't be guilt. Apart from anger, Ricardo didn't show emotion. Regret was never a part of his DNA.

Death soon replaced sulfur as he pushed the gun against the bed sheets. "You got lucky once, Steph. It ain't happening twice!"

He pulled the trigger three times but succumbed to the world of a thousand feathers.

"What the fuck?" he said, dropping the gun and stumbling backward.

Do it now, Mommy. Don't let me die for nothing.

I pressed the closet doors, but they were jammed again. There was no choice other than to kick them like a woman possessed. Both swung open, and Ricardo rushed me. But I pushed the blade deep into his neck. His arms spasmed. His lips moved. His words seemed to fail him. The bastard couldn't mutter a word.

My grip on the knife tightened as the steel tore through his throat. He dropped to his knees and raised a hand to his face. His soul was pale, his mind now damned. Ricardo softly gargled but didnt blink.

There was blood everywhere.

"I got lucky?" I asked as the encroaching moonlight crept through the gap in the curtains. "You don't know me as well as you think. I'm the bitch who makes her own luck."

I gritted my teeth and pushed the blade through his throat and into his jaw. Two twists and a push. The blade bounced off his skull and exited the back of his head. "Everybody loves a twist," I said, wiping his blood from my face.

I pushed him backward, and he slumped against the wall. "This is fun. It's a blast. What's up, asshole? Don't you want to play? You appear to have gone shy. Either that or you're stunned by my weapon of choice. You recognize it, don't you? It's the one you used to kill my baby. You killed her, Ricardo. You destroyed my Heidi."

I paused to the silence. That wasn't entirely true. I could hear Ricardo's shallow breath.

"That was for Sapphire," I said, fighting the tears. "She says hello. Why did you do it to us, Ricardo? I loved you. I'd have given anything to stand at your side. I did give everything, but you left me for dead. I did die. My world will never be the same. It's all because of you. I am a woman scorned."

A burning sensation trickled down my cheeks. "You took away the only thing precious to me. You killed Heidi. You killed me. You left me to die at the fucking swamp, asshole! "Only cowards hit women." Isn't that what you once said? James is a real man, but we'll talk about him later. In the meantime, it's the moment to extend those greetings."

Six inches of pent-up anger pierced the heart he never had. I felt weak, yet had the strength to curl that blade again, again, and again.

"And it's goodbye from Heidi. She thinks you're boring. You're the complete opposite of James. Oops, there I go again. What follows is courtesy of yours truly. Sweet dreams, loverboy. You can take those cowardly ways to hell."

I sliced off his nose as he gargled for one last time. Shallow became non-existent, and this was brutality at its finest. I stabbed him eighteen times in the chest and his face. It may have been thirty-one. I wasn't sure. Math had never been my strong point.

"Nobody takes on Stephanie Black and lives to tell the tale. Hearing me, dumbass? Why do I bother? You're mentally weak. You're insane. You left me to die."

There hadn't been an hour when I'd not fantasized about this moment. I wanted to celebrate. I wanted to throw the biggest shindig Texas had ever seen, but I dropped to my knees and sobbed. I'd taken the wolf to slaughter, but it shouldn't have come to this. "Why did you destroy my Heidi?"

I briefly closed my eyes and thought about that swamp. I should have let him bleed out. I should have made that bastard suffer until he could cry no more.

"Quit looking at me that way," I said, waving the blade at what remained of his face. "Didn't I tell you to stop looking at me? It's no time for ignorance. Okay, here it comes. Don't say I offered no warning." I popped out his eyes with the tip of the blade.

We almost finished, Mommy?

"Won't be long, precious. I'll introduce your father to my new toy. Milo and Dash, get your ass here right now." I took the saw from beneath the bed. The one I'd purchased earlier in the day. "Come on, boys. It's dinnertime."

Both sped into the room and began to paw at his eyes. Those mutts would have made great soccer players if it wasn't for their shaggy hair and incredibly large teeth. Dash pushed one toward Milo, but it went an inch before stopping in the gunk. Did June and Burt ever entertain them?

"Winner, winner, the dogs will have dinner."

I beamed when I heard the rap on the door. "Ms. Black, it's Chip Conroy," came a voice from beyond the wood. "I'm leading the watch tonight. I saw the lights go out and thought I'd check how you're doing."

My bloodied steps took me to the front door, and I couldn't help but giggle. "Everything's fine," I said. "I'm naked and about to crawl into the shower. The generator needs a restart, and who would have thought modern technology could be so unpredictable? I'm okay, but thanks for your concern."

I flicked the switch on the generator, which was to the left of the door. My eyes fleetingly strained at the surrounding brightness.

"I'm here if you need me," he added.

"And I feel so much safer in your presence," I sarcastically replied. "Keep up the great work, and God bless America. Oh, and before I forget. I'll make you guys some breakfast in the morning. I don't have much by way of groceries, but I can rustle up some sandwiches. Trust me. They're to die for."

His steps became distant.

Although painful, I skipped back to the bedroom. It was more of a hobble than a skip, and I stared hard at his sorry ass. "It's you and me, Ricardo. No more interruptions. How exciting is that? I'll show you how cutting I can be."

I took his wrists and pulled him toward the basement door.

It was a struggle, but I got there eventually. "You're not fat, but you've piled on the kilos," I muttered. "You could have burned so many calories if you didn't piss me off. What doesn't kill you makes you stronger, right? Oops, it's too late. Don't move. I'll need a little wine for the next bit."

I sluggishly went to the kitchen. I didn't bother with the glass and grabbed the whole freaking bottle.

I returned moments later, opened the basement door, and rolled him down the steps. I locked the door behind me. A bottle of red, a hungry saw, and somebody deserving of such refined companionship?

The night was beyond perfect.

His skull went crack, he broke his little back, and all the dark corruption cried, Black, Black, Black. I like nursery rhymes, Mommy.

"And I'll read you one every night, princess."

The electric saw was quieter than I thought it would be. It was sharper, too, and the next three hours saw me strip every last inch of flesh from his body. I separated bone from meat, and both found a home inside two steel drums I often used for the laundry.

Are we finished, Mommy? I want to play with the black roses in the garden.

I thought about Oscar as my heavy stare caught sight of one of those drums. "Okay, it's the moment to talk about James. I've got a confession to make, but I'll break it to you gently. I'm falling for the guy."

There came a soft, but tingling silence.

"He delivers waves of excitement through my body without touching me. He'll be the daddy you could never be. Oscar will want for nothing, but don't let the news rip you apart."

I again stopped to inhale the tranquility of the cabin. "I forgot to ask, silly me. Could you quit calling me Steph? You know I hate that name."

His cooking flesh smelled disgusting, and it was a lousy time to have run out of seasoning. Milo and Dash enjoyed it raw. I didn't realize those mangy mutts could eat so much. There were lots left over, but tomorrow was another day.

Ricardo was so predictable.

CHAPTER TWENTY

December 24, 2017

I was early to rise, which made for a change. My sleeping patterns had been out of whack since those head-piercing migraines, the morning sickness, and what felt like an eternal stay at Greenfields Hospital.

Knowing I wouldn't open my eyes to a potential threat made life bearable again.

The coast appeared clear, so I pushed the wheelbarrow and a bag of compost to the back of the garden. It was the moment to get busy.

What would become a bed of roses soon doubled up as a burial ground for a murdering bastard. I was discreet—undeniably so—yet fortunate that those watching had their eyes elsewhere. Bones and Roses? It almost sounded like the most incredible band in the world.

Concealing a little of the evidence was easier than I thought, although the basement took me hours to clean.

Minutes later, I placed a large plate of sandwiches on the hood of a Dodge. "Morning, boys," I waved. "I've made breakfast as a gesture of appreciation. You were amazing last night, and I don't know what I'd have done without you."

Chase stepped out of one of those cars. "There's been an interesting development, Ms. Black," he said, reaching for a sandwich. "It's great news."

"You have me intrigued," I returned, "but what happened to the other car? I could have sworn there were four. I recall counting them."

I winced as one of his colleagues took a bite of his sandwich. "These are incredible," he said, helping himself to a second. "It's like pork but sharper."

"Sorry, Captain Chase, I hate to be blunt, but what's this news?" I asked, trying to contain the laughter.

"Yeah, the fourth car. Your original tail had links to de Souza, so they're currently at the precinct. If that connection's confirmed, those cops will be dealt with in the sternest way imaginable."

"And the news?"

"There ain't no reason for us to be here anymore," he returned, running his long, fat fingers through his hair. "De Souza's dead. We think he is, anyway."

I gazed toward the back of the garden. "No, Ricardo wouldn't make it so easy. People like him don't die. What makes you think he's dead?"

"It ain't confirmed, but they found some of his things in and around the Missouri River. A fisherman hooked in his blue jacket. His badge, a service pistol, socks, and a pair of muddy boots were found a short while later. Who else goes swimming in December? Seems conclusive if you ask me."

I shielded my eyes from the beating rays of another beautiful day. "And his body?"

"We're still combing the area. It'll take some time."

"Isn't he still alive until they find him?" I smiled when casting a second glance toward the rose bush. It was growing by the breath. "I don't want him dead," I admitted. "I want him to face a jury for what he did to us that night. And you're still searching, right?"

"It's over two thousand miles long, and that dirty rat could be in any stretch of that river. We'll search our jurisdiction, but it's as far as we go. Can I ask why you planted flowers in the garden just minutes ago?"

"I was burying Ricardo," I laughed. "Sorry, that was my lame attempt at humor. Trauma and relief can make you say the silliest of things. It's a memorial for Heidi. We weren't together for long, yet our bond will remain forever. Is that June? It is."

Burt's blue Chevy parked alongside me, and June opened the door. She immediately planted her filthy boots on the rich, dark soil. "Howdy, neighbor," she said, flashing me a smile. "I hope they behaved themselves."

"I wouldn't have known they were there. I'll fetch them, and you can say your goodbyes."

I opened the cabin door seconds later, and Milo and Dash sped across the dusty, winding path. Their tails wagged excitedly in a moment's breeze.

But then things went awry. They knocked June off her feet and began to savage her leg. "Burt, get them off me!" she screamed. "Please get—Milo. Dash. No!"

She tried to fight them off, arms flailing, her cries pleading for help. That help was slow to come. We were too shocked to say or do anything, and the more June fought, the more ferocious those canines became.

Three of her fingers disappeared into the clutches of Milo's jaws, and I internally apologized as I saw blood dripping from his mouth.

Chase dragged them away before drawing his gun. Two shots. Two yelps.

Silence seemed to hang in the air for eternity. They were ugly mutts, but that didn't mean I wanted to see them suffer.

Very clever, Mommy. There goes a bit more of the evidence.

"Could you get her to a hospital?" Burt said, unsure if he should cuddle the dead or the wounded. "It don't look deep, but it's gotta be cleared of infections. You got lights. You'll get there faster." He put the dogs in the back of his truck.

The place soon cleared, but Chase and I remained. I was about to thank the captain when I saw him smile at the gorgeous scarlet-red Buick to the west. It may have been the first time he'd shown such emotion.

"You got one last surprise," he said, clipping his sunglasses to his jacket.

My cane fell to the ground as a woman climbed out of the stunning car. "Sapphire?" I said, questioning my sanity. "It's not possible. You're supposed to be dead."

She emitted warmth when squeezing my hands. "Vic and I are childhood sweethearts," she told me. "I'm real, honey bunches. I'm alive. Mallory came for me, but Vic beat him to the punch. That sonofabitch fled when he saw who he was up against."

"But how?" I was more confused than ever, yet it was so amazing to see her.

"There was a greater chance of catching Ricardo if he thought I was dead. Vic was able to put all of his resources on your ass. I wanted to tell you, but he thought it was too dangerous. I guess the attention wasn't needed after all. Ricardo was all hat, no cattle."

"I'm sorry for what happened that night," I said, my eyes fixed on the ground. "I was powerless to do anything."

"You saved my life. I'm forever in your debt. Did you order a hotdog?"

"It's James," I beamed excitedly. "He's the ultimate guy."

He leaned out of the window and coughed away the returning smoke. I detected a theme. "You ready?" James asked, taking off his white hat and throwing it behind him. "Amanda gave me the boot, so we get to spend most of the day together. Sorry. Hi, people."

James sounded stupid, but he was my stupid, at least for the day.

"It appears somebody hit the jackpot," Sapphire said, gently nudging my ribs with her elbow. "That boy's a hoot. He won't have two dimes to rub together, but who cares when you wake up next to a face like that? He's almost as dashing as Vic."

I gave her the biggest hug ever. "How about we catch up soon?" I asked. "Perhaps we could take a trip to Austin as a four? We can shop until we drop before letting the boys treat us to a wonderful meal. We'll exchange stories. Oh, and you'll so love the rosebush I'm creating. It's only a *skeleton* of a flowerbed, but it will be beautiful once it's bloomed."

"I'm sold," Sapphire laughed. "When we're finished, how about we hit a nightclub? We can show the world how cougars can boogie as well as the rest of them."

"Oi, cheeky."

Chase offered me his hand, and I didn't hesitate to shake it. "We're planning on getting hitched in the spring," he nodded. "Here's hoping we see you there. Oh, and you ain't to forget that help."

"Thanks, Captain Chase. We wouldn't miss it for the world. Just make sure your beautiful bride-to-be throws the bouquet my way," I winked.

I climbed into the hot dog van and strapped on my belt. "Where are we going, partner?" I asked, almost embarrassed by what was arguably the biggest pile of junk in Texas.

"It's yours, Stephanie. The world's your lobster. Any news on de Souza?"

"I no longer care about the guy. I never did, but I've been

meaning to ask. Do you like kids?"

"Yeah, but I couldn't eat a whole one. Nah, seriously. I'm all for having a family, but I'm only young. Maybe in ten—"

"Months?" I timed my interruption to perfection. "Do you like the cabin? What you said last night got me thinking. Why don't you move in? It's rent-free, and you can save for our wedding. I don't mean to be forward. I know what I want, but I don't usually get it."

Stephanie Trapp was such a magical name, and I was finally living amid the most beautiful fairytale. James was my dream, and nobody would ever steal him away. I'd been scorned once, and it wouldn't happen twice.

He wasn't the only one that had me excited. I thought about that nightmare at the swamp. There remained a score to be settled.

Hi, Merv. We're going to play a game. It's called hide, and hide some more.

PART TWO

CHAPTER ONE

December 24, 2018

A year had passed since Ricardo was taught a lesson in the harshest way imaginable. Life had moved on, and it was no longer about him. James was the most incredible person I'd ever met and I couldn't wait until we married in the fall.

I had to survive the day, and it was the most exciting one ever. It was the day of my next appointment and nothing had changed. I desperately wanted that baby to call my own.

My results would be fruitful, and I'd be given the all-clear to have the third and final test.

But it brought trepidation in abundance, and most of my nights were spent waking up in a puddle of sweat. I'd revisit that swamp and smell the stench of rotten eggs. I'd also inhale the sulfur as it clung to my weak, slight breath.

I should have been dead, yet those dreams always made me feel alive.

I'd hear tiny feet skipping around the cabin as if to play hide and seek. I could never play the other game. Not with baby Oscar. I could only play it with a soul, now damned.

In the penultimate stage of my dreams, Ricardo and Merv hovered regretfully at the bottom of the bed. I believed in the paranormal, yet I had no idea why the latter was there. Rumor said he was confined to four crooked wheels and a rusted bedpan.

Merv was one year slower. It made him one year closer to death.

He didn't know it, but Hurricane Black would soon be on the offensive. My destination would be an old rundown shack called Coffin Willow. It was a click away from Baldwin.

But now wasn't the time to act in haste. I had so much energy about me, yet I had to use it wisely. At the top of the list came the most fantastic guy ever created.

I looked to my left and couldn't help but bite my lip. Then I thanked the brightness of the moon for what it'd given me. James, wow. What a gorgeous smile. He had the face of an untainted angel.

I love how he slept wearing nothing but his flesh, and it was so damn easy to ride at the rodeo. The bull would be defeated. It always was, and now was no exception.

His eyes remained shut as he gently reached for my hips. "No, Stephanie. We should use protection."

"Is that what you want?" I leaned back and took hold of his ankles.

"It won't work like this." Although his feeble attempt to push me off him was doomed for failure, his childlike smile almost cut me in two. "We plan this right."

"What's there to plan?" I asked, grinding him to submission. "Boy meets girl. Both play… oh, yeah. Both play and nine months later…"

He slipped out of the rodeo and sat up, back straight. "You know what I'm talking about. What time is it? Gone six. Great. I love you, but I need to crash." James fell backward before burying his head beneath the pillow. "I hate it when you drop this shit on me so early in the morning."

"But it's the perfect moment to practice," I said, gently pulling at the soft silk sheets.

"Every minute of the day is your perfect moment to practice. You had five of them yesterday, three the day before that, and eight if you care to go that bit further. I'm exhausted, baby."

"You're young and energetic."

"I'm not a performing puppy dog. It's late. It's dark, so don't spout any of that fantasy bullshit. I've promised you… wait… how many… yeah, three hundred and sixty-six times that we'll start that family, but not yet. Be patient."

I jumped off the bed and stormed to the closet. "Then when? I'm not getting any younger, James. Even cougars have an expiration date."

"Please don't smack those hangers against the—listen, I want this family. There's nothing I want more, but we can't rush things. You said it yourself. The account has limited cash, and this job will change everything."

"James?"

"No, Stephanie. I have the interview in a few hours, so you should see the snowball form at the top of the hill. I'll clear a hundred big ones a year, and we can have as many babies as we want. Mom stays at home while Dad earns the corn. C'mon, beautiful. I've asked you to stop clanging those hangers. You did that on purpose."

And it was only going to get louder. "It shouldn't be about money. This is all about love."

"That's life," James shrugged. "Apart from a stunning cabin in the middle of nowhere and a little cash from de Souza's payout, you get nothing for free. I still can't believe you were the sole beneficiary of his will."

I shook my head and rolled my eyes. "It was twenty thousand, so don't make it sound more. Oh, and don't mention him anywhere. You know how—what if my eggs are the problem?" My eyes welled up at the thought as I returned to the bed. "Being a malfunction to life would haunt me. Maybe my body is failing me. Maybe I'm the failure."

His arms immediately became a cloak for my shoulders, and James dropped warm, tender kisses on my naked flesh. "It'll be fine," he said, soft and assuring. "The omens are good. You passed the first with flying kites, and the second looks nailed. Remember what you said about your vibe?"

"Yes, but—"

"No buts," James laughed. "You've bounced around the cabin for days. I've heard you whistle and sing, and I didn't know a person could smile so much without getting a cramp on their face." Our fingers intertwined. "This can only mean one thing. Trust me, Stephanie. Trust yourself. We're almost there."

"You're right," I said. "I'm being silly. Dr. Forlorn will tell me what an amazing parent I'll be and how Oscar is lucky to have such an incredible mom. I can't wait, but I'm so damn nervous. Will they tell me today? How do people deal with the trauma? I guess it's possible, scientifically, although the clinic isn't the most efficient of places. How amazing it would be if I could travel in time."

"Stephanie?"

"Huh?"

James was now gripping my elbows. "You're driving me insane. Just relax. Things will work out. Oh, and while we're on the subject, we should talk about the baby's name. I thought our first would be called Heidi. I swear it was what you told me a while back."

"Our baby will be a boy. If he was there, I could almost feel him kick." I felt for James' face and thumbed the sleep away from his eyes. "It has to be Oscar. Don't make me explain why."

It won't be long, Mommy. I'll be the best boy ever.

I was praying my demons would show me the way.

"How are you feeling?" I asked, remembering our stint in the bathroom.

"I'm okay now. Whatever I ate disagreed with me, and I was vomiting for hours."

"We both were, remember?" I returned, "but I'm also feeling okay. Thanks for your concern."

"I'm sorry. I didn't mean to sound selfish."

I momentarily tripped back to that gas station. It was the same station I'd visited when purchasing that electrical saw. I often drove to Scottsville, so it was my regular place to buy groceries. Whenever I stopped at that cemetery, something would ignite in my stomach. What followed were the sparks of warmth and happiness.

"Could it have been the vegetables?" I asked, pulling a face of utter disgust. "The more I think about it, the more I realize it's not the cleanest place in the world."

"Can we do this a little later?" James replied, again slamming the pillow down to his face. "I'm trying to sleep."

"No, James, let's do it now. I'll never return there if he's sold us rotten mushrooms. They looked—wait, could it have been the steaks?"

"You're driving me insane!" James said.

"I didn't even recognize the sauce. Why did beef taste like bitter pork? You did go to the butcher, right? I told you to get the meat from the butcher. Tell me you listened for once."

"Yeah, about that meat."

I felt my eyebrows bounce off the ceiling. "Tell me the truth, James. Did you or did you not get the meat from the butcher?"

"Not quite. I was clearing out the freezer when I stumbled on gold. I thought we could save some—"

"No, James. I don't want to hear this right now. Tell me you never took the meat from the freezer!"

"It took an age to defrost, but it got there in the—"

"You don't cook, James," I said, feeling my face drain of life. "You've never cooked since the first day we met. You shouldn't be even going into the—listen to the question and answer it, will you? Did you take the meat from the freezer?"

"Yeah, I took it from the... Stephanie, what's wrong?"

I sprinted into the bathroom, and the next hour saw me throw up my guts! I hated Ricardo. In life or death, that bastard would haunt me regardless.

CHAPTER TWO

James dressed, his handsome reflection bouncing off the beautifully crafted, tall, convex mirror. He could raise the temperature in an arctic freeze.

A part of me never wanted him to strike gold at his interview. It was selfish, I know, but failure would mean us spending more time together.

But then I'd think of the bigger picture. If James got the job with CJA Marketing, he'd always wear that suit. It was weird why his interview was on Christmas Eve, but I guess he'd been head-hunted in case Insane Hamburger Incorporation came requesting his services.

I loved him so damn much. He was hotter than lava.

"Getting dressed today?" he asked, reaching for his ties.

"Heard anything from Bobby? You know, the brother I've never had the pleasure of meeting. Christmas Day is one helluva time to be formally introduced."

"He's shacked up with a girl he met at work," James replied. "I'll never be a priority. He was supposed to call yesterday, but he must be busy. Bobby said there was a surprise, but don't ask what it is. Knowing him, he's probably married a stranger in Vegas. He can be spontaneous like that. He used to be in his younger days."

I stood there, shaking my head. "You should call him. I need to know how many I'm cooking for."

"There's a storm in Dallas," he told me, reaching for his silver-blue tie. "Communications are currently down. I can call Mom in New Hampshire. I could speak to an uncle in Utah, but their network hasn't been hit by an act of God. They're working on it, but it's Christmas Eve, Stephanie. They're probably struggling to put a team together. Just chill. Cook for four, and we'll see who turns up."

He was all thumbs and fingers, and I always had to fix his tie. It was adorable.

"Dallas has had three network outages this week," I returned. "This smells more like incompetence than an act of God. It's a word I know too well. It's been around me since the day I was born. Anyway, workers can only be called such a thing if they, umm, work."

"You're obsessed with my brother," James said, putting on his cufflinks. "Bobby's not the most reliable guy you'll meet, and don't be surprised if he turns up on the doorstep. It's how he rolls."

"You don't talk about him much. Has he got the same dashing looks as you?"

"Are we still talking about my bro? We drifted after I moved to this part of Texas, but it happens. You grow up and have your own shit to shovel. We're peas in a pod, with one or two similarities." His smile was so damn adorable.

I took my lucky white dress from the closet and pressed it against my body. It remained a perfect fit. "I'll soon be heading to the clinic," I told him. "There's an appointment to attend. Time permitting, I may head into Lodi after I'm done."

James nodded as he again checked himself in the mirror. "Yeah, I love you, too."

"Can you see tiny blue zebras dancing on my nose?" I sarcastically asked.

"I've told you already. Communications are down."

My hand felt for the back of my head, and I had to know what galaxy he'd drifted to. "Are you listening?" I asked, removing my slippers. "I'll be popping into Lodi as three Hispanic guys want to ravish me in a luxurious motel room. I can't wait."

"Yeah, the weather looks great. They say it'll be another hot one."

He managed to duck as my slipper whizzed past his ear. "Do you ever listen, or is it another wonderful trait the male inherits at birth?" I said, eyeing up my second slipper. "I've got to collect the turkey after the clinic, so is there anything else you want me to pick up?"

There was a twinkle in his eye. It was one I'd seen on numerous occasions. "Wouldn't say no to another gift," he batted back after considering the question. "You should treat yourself to a sexy little number while you're—"

"How about we deal?" I said, knowing it was the moment to negotiate. "Promise me what I desire most, and I'll pick up something beyond your wildest fantasies."

He finally clipped on his cufflinks before giving me one of those thigh-trembling smiles. "What time are you back?" he asked.

"Do we have time to finish what we started?" I replied, living in hope. "Okay, I get it. Another time. When am I back? Does it matter? Hey, I hope you're not sneaking home a mistress."

My second slipper hit him flush on the mouth, so I paced across the room and slapped him with a hundred kisses. "I'm so sorry. I didn't think I was capable of hitting you."

James playfully put me over his shoulder before dropping me to the bed. "You can't have pleasure without pain." Our lips smacked, and my heart was doing somersaults. "I love you, Stephanie. I'm wildly in love with you, and there won't ever be another. Why touch cotton when silk runs through your soul?"

"Nice save but be careful of that suit. You shouldn't crease it before your stupid interview. Can I rip it off and have my devilish way with you?" I again bit my lip.

He pushed my hands against the pillow, and I conceded to his dominant ways. "But this will have to wait until tonight," he frowned. "It's a busy day for the both of us."

"Can't you come with me?" I found myself almost pleading.

"I always do," he shot back. "It's the things you do to—"

"Quit screwing around," I sharply returned. "Reschedule the interview, and come with me, James. My appointment's far more important than yours. It is to me. It should be for the both of us."

He sat up and slipped into his flat black shoes. "I get it, Stephanie. You want a kid. It's not like you talk about anything else, but I'll soon be in Rodessa. It's where the magic begins."

"The least you could do is support me," I said, arms folded. "Forlorn says it's possible that you could have a problem."

"I thought those tests went well?" he asked, rising to his feet.

"They did, but he also wants to run a few tests on you. You'll need to give him—"

"There's nothing wrong with my swimmers," he cut in. "Don't you watch the news? There are reports that every last one of my dudes is an Olympic gold medalist."

I slipped into my gorgeous white dress. "Please cancel, just this once. I'd feel special if I knew I was your top priority."

"You're always my priority. If you've not realized by now, you never will." He kissed me on the forehead before stepping out of the bedroom.

James tended to frustrate me, and I wished he'd grow up and take responsibility. I needed solidity. I was beginning to believe he was in fear of answers he never wanted to hear.

I followed him into the lounge, and he perched in front of the TV.

"Anything on those power outages?" I asked, sitting down beside him.

"Not yet, but I only put it on a minute ago. There's been no mention of Dallas whatsoever."

"I could use your support today. Please, James."

"How many times do we have to talk about this?" he said, vigorously shaking his head. "I can't pull shit like that at the drop of a hat. Life doesn't work that way."

"You would if you loved me."

"Don't treat me like a bitch," he shot back. "Emotional blackmail gets you nowhere. Buck Kruiger's already left Sacramento, and we're scheduled to meet this afternoon. We could hit the jackpot. The world will be our oyster. Oh, and you look sensational."

I grabbed the controller and turned off the TV. Dimness now encompassed us. "Why must it be about money?" I asked, rising to my feet. "It would be nice if you put our happiness first."

"Who bought you the Versace? What about those Christian Louboutin shoes, the Gucci purses, and the brand-new Audi? Some of that's on credit. Our credit, but we won't survive without green. It's the reality of life, and you should occasionally get a grip on what's around you. Unless I catch this job, there won't be more of that stuff."

I got to my feet and blindly reached for my keys. "We're not doing this again, James. I'm not fighting today. I should go. One of us needs to make an effort at the clinic."

"Let me know how you get on. Everything will be perfect, you'll see. Oh, and I meant to ask. Is your mom coming over tomorrow?"

"I told her to stay clear."

"What's happened?" he dug in. "Stephanie, what have you done?"

"She frustrates the hell out of me. I went to see her yesterday, but we argued again. Mom's not happy about us getting hitched in the fall. She won't trust my choice of men. Mom thinks you're a nobody, but I told her to back off."

"And you left it like that?"

I tossed my keys in the air but failed to catch them. "We argued, but it's over. She's spending the entire day cooking for Pops. I call him Pops, but he's not my real parent. He married Mom after Dad was sent to prison."

"What did he do?" James asked, reaching for his olive-green jacket.

"He's earned the same treatment as Ricardo, only I didn't need to... I better go. See you later."

He pulled me into his arms. "I'll win your mom over, you'll see. How could she resist my charm?"

"You'll never need to impress anybody except our children and me," I said, bending down to pick up my keys. "Bye, James."

CHAPTER THREE

I stopped the car in an almost empty parking lot, and things felt incredibly strange. A low mist swept in from the south, a sky drabber than threatening. The whole world was gray… a twisted reversal of paradise.

But my finger began to tap at the wheel furiously. I had to break through the fear. Somehow, I had to conquer those demons and pass through my valley of darkness.

I fought valiantly for the light I once knew.

Seconds later, I inched through the swinging doors and sat on one of the many seats to my right. The place was dead except for a couple of happy-go-lucky nurses and a girl who irritatingly chewed gum behind the counter.

But along came the janitor, and the tranquility was broken. He began to mop the floor, his mouth a little too vocal for this ungodly hour. "And the bells are ringin' out for Christmas Day."

An irritant was murdering such a beautiful tune.

Think positive, Mommy. Have faith in that body of ours.

I again stared at the dozen vacant seats. What idiot in their right mind would be so desperate to book an appointment on Christmas Eve?

I looked at my watch again, again and again, but the hands weren't moving. The battery had died. Why did we even need watches when time was irrelevant? Why were they taking so long? There was so much to do.

"Umm, hello?" said the lady behind the counter. "Got an appointment?"

I despised anybody who chewed gum, and this girl probably had the same freaking stick since the day she was born. Despise was too strong a word. It was a special day, so all was forgiven. Her ridiculous black beehive hairstyle and low-cut lime bodycon had also found redemption.

"Umm, hello?" she said again, filing her nails.

"Oh, sorry, I'm here to see Dr. Forlorn." I scuttled over to the counter. "It's Black. Ms. Stephanie Black. I'm his nine-thirty."

"Dr. Forlorn will see you now. Down the corridor, and—"

"Yes, I've been here before."

"Here's hoping your wish arrives a day early and many more will be answered. Merry Christmas, Ms. Black. Don't keep the doctor waiting."

I gently nodded as I began the long walk to his office.

I turned but had to shield my eyes from the blinding shine. It bounced through the beautiful French windows, and those forecasters had nailed the weather again.

"Thank you," I said to the girl, acknowledging her kind words. "May I make an observation? It's important. It could shape your destiny."

"Umm, yeah," she said in confusion. "Go ahead."

"There's no ring on your finger, leading me to two possible conclusions. You're either the jealous bridesmaid, or you're out to impress. Are you a whore who swears by the laws of infidelity? I don't believe you are. You'd love to meet Mr. Right, but he'll never exist. Not while you have an asteroid of gum stuck in your mouth. You're beautiful. You will be if you lose the big red cross. May you and your family have a wonderful Christmas."

She spat her gum into the bin.

I made the walk but stood terrified as I gazed ominously at the door. I so desperately wanted to open it but couldn't. It wasn't the handle I feared nor the pine that offered an alternative dimension. It was everything fated to come after.

My palms were drenched in an ocean of coward's sweat, yet I eventually reached for the brass. I had to lose the emotion to beat those demons, but how was that possible? Most fears could be cured, yet there was never a fix for failure.

Judgment day had arrived. It sure wouldn't let me forget it.

Things will be fine. You'll see.

I stepped inside, my hands violently shaking.

CHAPTER FOUR

Forlorn sat in his chair, his off-white gown almost covering his knees. He smiled. I think he did, and that was a positive. I crossed my fingers, and this had to be the best news ever.

"Morning, Ms. Black," he said, pointing to the leather chair before him. "Take a seat. There's much to discuss. Firstly, let me tell you how happy I am that you made the appointment. I know how busy and stressful December can be, and my wife hasn't stopped decorating since—"

"I've been good, but thanks for asking," I returned, my hands gripping the chair. "I don't mean to be blunt, but could we start the third test? There's so much to do; James even promised to help me put up a tree this evening. I'm sure he said that, although I could be wrong. It wouldn't be the first time. It's a Norwegian spruce."

"And it'll look beautiful standing tall in your living room."

He began to flick through my file, but it felt like he was reading one page an hour. Even that freaking hotdog van was quicker than this. "Can we move this along?" I asked, pushing my ass to the edge of the chair.

"Yes, about that third test." He looked me in the eye before his gaze returned to the page. "I'm afraid it's not good news."

My stomach did somersaults on the fluffy carpet. "Can we begin?" The anxiety continued to chew away at my guts, as his words hit me harder than I've ever been hit before.

"What are you telling me?" The room became dim. The

tables, those chairs, and the doctor were levitating at the apex of a black hole. A void that instantly made my body tremble in fear.

Black never looked so dark.

"There won't be a third test. It's never easy to deliver such news, but the results were not what we hoped for."

"No, you have this—I know my constitutional rights. I demand my third test. I demand it's done immediately."

I sank into the chair as my throat became a scorched desert in a shattered chasm. "I'm not listening. I'll go to church tonight. There's plenty of time, but I'm not religious. It's nothing like that. I like to thirst on his blood. You know, the wine. It's cheaper than buying the crap from a liquor store."

Forlorn reached for my hands, his face empty of emotion. "I'd like nothing more than to give you the news you so desperately seek, but I can't. It would only be a—"

"I can be fixed, right? We can patch up a rocket in space. You have people spinning around the Titanic in funky submarines, so tell me what to do. It's important. I need to know about the Christmas tree. What time do we get the blood? The wine. I don't need help."

He sighed when sucking in a breath. Was it a sigh or a laugh? "Having a child is impossible due to the historical damage to your womb," he softly said, "but it's not the end of the world. We should run through your options." His grip on my fingers tightened.

I was a failure of procreation. I was fated to suffer a lifetime of indignity in hell.

"Why must I again grieve because of what he did to me?" I asked, staring at the flick of his silver hair. "Why do I get to carry a cross of my eternal shame? Those results are wrong. Someone screwed up. It's incompetence!"

"About those other avenues," he said, letting go of my hands. "You should consider—"

"Other avenues? Okay, I'm calm. I'm listening. Breathe, Stephanie, breathe. Shoot. Tell me how we make this right."

"Adoption's more common than you think. You should—"

"Are you insane?" I snapped, standing up and stepping away from his desk. I thought I was going to fall through the floor. "Please don't hit me with such bullcrap. I'm a failure. I don't want to be a failure, but that's what I am. Why am I a goddamn failure? I never wanted to fail."

I dropped my purse to the floor. It took nine attempts to retrieve it.

Forlorn again took hold of my hands. "It's clear how traumatized you are, Ms. Black. It's understandable, but you should think about the options. Many children need a loving home. You can be their mainstay. You can achieve something special by being such a wonderful mom. You can even be on the line and watch your daughter play soccer."

"It's a boy. Let's get one thing straight. I have a boy in my pouch. His name's Oscar."

"Apologies, Ms. Black. Oscar will tell his teacher what an incredible parent you are. Tell his teacher how lucky he is to have such an amazing mom. But unfortunately, he won't be your biological child."

Why was he telling me this? I could have slapped him. I'd have probably done so if I wasn't numb.

"Did I mention surrogacy?" he added.

"No, it's impossible. I can't do it. I can't do surrogacy or adoption. I have to pick up the turkey. I have vegetables to prepare for tomorrow. My day is about to get busy."

"Ms. Black, please take a moment to digest the news. I can

see the psychological effect it's had on you, so allow me to refer you to a dear friend of mine. We'll act immediately. Dr. Charles Butcher is the best in his—"

"My body tingles," I interrupted, pinching my hands. "I feel strange. My heart skips beats, doctor. What's happening to me?"

He leaned forward. I think it was forward, although it may have been back. "If you could sign here, here, and here. We need your permission to make that referral."

"Didn't you hear what I said?" I returned, rubbing my temples. "It's out of the question. No, just no."

"It's a hammer blow," he muttered, dropping his pen to the desk. "An exploding bomb when you should be rejoicing in the birth of our Lord. It is what it is. You're a fucking failure. You'll never have a child to call your own. It's hilarious. Get out. Please go. This is a chamber for success, not collapse. Stephanie Black is a malfunction to life!"

I rose to my feet, my steps silently leading me to the door. But then I turned for one last time. "Sorry, what did you say?"

"I apologized for being the one who dropped the—please think about that help."

The darkest chill ran up my spine, and a thousand scorpions covered me. They pinched me. They hurt me. They attacked in great numbers.

Time passed, and I sat in my Audi, wondering when I'd left the clinic behind.

My fingers played the sequel on the wheel, yet I didn't realize I'd been hitting it so hard. Blood dripped to my wrists and came to puddle on my white beautiful dress. I was covered in the stuff.

What was wrong with me?

CHAPTER FIVE

Forlorn never understood me, and no man ever had. I recalled Ricardo saying something similar about himself last year. He was wrong. His card had already been marked, and it had been that way since he left me to die in the swamp.

I could never adopt. He could never be mine. I needed a baby born out of love, want, and happiness. I wanted one to call my own flesh and blood.

Ricardo had so much to answer for. He'd destroyed my perfect fantasy. I didn't realize it then, but the day I met him was when I'd inherited a hex on my shoulder. He'd placed another in my womb the night I cut him into tiny bits no bigger than a thumb.

"Damn you, Ricardo! Why did you have to do those things? Damn you for eternity."

There came a knock on the window. "You okay, lady?"

I stared into the eyes of the passerby. I tried, but they were blocked by his shades and his red, low-rimmed cap. His poodle was taking a piss on my wheel. Was it a dog? Perhaps it was a kite or a baby. A baby?

"Why can you have one, but I can't?" I slapped the dash repeatedly. "And tell it to quit messing on my wheel. Answer me, asshole. Was there a question? No, there wasn't. Won't you answer the goddamn question?"

He paced away but stopped by the clinic and reached for his phone. He pointed toward me, his jaw now touching the ground.

I kicked the car into motion and couldn't help but think about Marshall Mincemeat. If only he were alive. I could bury that bastard again, again, and again. He was the immortal hex in my womb.

Eighty-seven.

Ninety.

Ninety-four.

I couldn't slow down. I couldn't do anything except grieve for a past I once knew. I needed to be home with James. I had to feel the warmth and be wrapped in his love. He'd tell me everything would be okay. It would be, but I could never adopt.

Hot, raging infernos replaced the coldness of the tears. Piece by piece, they burned away at my broken spirit. I heard no crackle. Just the echoes of hounds feasting on my soul.

Mental turbulence was replaced by a siren in the distance. It was possibly two. Most definitely, four. They shrieked. All five cried out in pain, but it magnetized my foot to the pedal. A hundred never felt so slow.

Perhaps they weren't sirens. They were helicopters and hazelnuts. That's what they were. I caught the unmistakable whiff of charred pork and laughed when I imagined myself standing in Ricardo's puddle of shiny red blood.

Fond memories could never die old.

But that crap wasn't for me. Not anymore. I may have fleetingly lost control back then, yet those cracks had finally sealed. I was calm. I was serene. I was the soft breeze that found its haven amid the most beautiful golden sunset.

But my white dress was now a deadly shade of red. I loved the tranquility.

It wasn't long before I was lying up alongside the cabin.

Things remained silent, and I couldn't even hear the click of a cricket's cry.

How long has passed since I left the clinic behind? It felt like an age. Two ages, yet it had to be seconds ago. It didn't matter. I had to pull myself together, regardless.

My pace took me to the rosebush. I needed to be here, just for a while. I had to damn this fool for eternity.

"You made a mistake when taking on Stephanie Black," I snarled. "You paid the heaviest price. I did it for Heidi. I did it for Sapphire. I did it for every girl you've attacked or hurt. Nobody will find you. You took a swim in the Missouri, remember? You're a forgotten soul. It's all you'll ever be. I've moved on, and you're zapped from my mind."

I turned and gazed confusingly toward the SUV parked at the side of the cabin. I must have passed it en route, but it didn't register. It was green, although yellow sprung to mind. Perhaps it was orange. No, it was undoubtedly gray. Gray with a hint of red.

"Don't you dare go anywhere, you murdering sonofabitch! Life is about to get busy. Don't wait up, loverboy."

I headed toward the blue SUV.

It was stunning and new, yet I'd never seen it before. It wasn't the forgettable type. Even the little sticker on the window was cute. A canine throwing balls of fire. I'd seen that image before, but where? How interesting.

I pushed open the door. "James? Is that you, James?"

My call was diluted to that of a whisper.

There came a noise to my left. My pulse should have beat drums, yet I remained calm and at ease. Was another of Ricardo's friends desperately needing a dish best served cold? Who else could it be? James was supposed to be out for the day.

CHAPTER SIX

I snuck into the kitchen, and my thin, trembling fingers slipped inside the coldness of the drawer. Who'd be dumb enough to enter my goddamn castle without permission?

I reached for a knife, and an eruption of heat instantly sunk into the palm of my hand. It was the same knife I'd used to slice through Ricardo's windpipe.

One blade was missing. It wasn't as big or ugly as the steel I now held, but I could have sworn it was there yesterday.

Skin-pinching chills waved up the back of my legs. Where was the gun? James wanted to hunt with a friend, so I bought him a rifle as a birthday gift. I think it was a rifle. I asked him to put it in the basement, but did he listen? No guy ever did.

I should have called Chase before leaving the cabin. I'd seen this a thousand times in the movies. The caller was the victim, and it was never anything different. I couldn't leave. I couldn't abandon those controlling demons.

I refused to be a fatality twice on the same day.

I found myself in the basement. I hadn't physically moved, yet here I was. And then I saw it. The rifle was on the shelf. The gift. I loved it when James got me. I loved how he always listened.

Was it loaded, and where did the bullets go? It didn't matter. I had power. To have was to hold. They'd see their destiny before running for the hills. I lived in hope.

You should leave, Mommy. We need to be safe.

With the rifle in my right hand and a knife in my left, I limped to the front door. It was the first time I'd felt such physical pain since crawling through the swamp an eternity ago.

I again thought about leaving, but there was business to attend.

There came a bang. There were two, and then a female voice shook me to the core. "Yes! Oh, God, yes. Harder. I'm close!"

I stared at the blue lace panties, the brown suede boots, a pair of blue denim, and a glittering silver tank top.

My heart immediately froze when I realized they were a trail to my bedroom. They weren't my size or color, and things were so confusing.

"Don't stop, baby!" she shouted. "Grab my ass and hit me with that hotdog!"

Her cries of ecstasy reverberated through my brain. It was my cabin. My bedroom. I made the rules. How could James do this to me? How could he destroy my world so soon after my maternal dream had been shattered?

My legs were heavy. I felt weak and unbalanced, so I leaned against the wooden wall and stared at that lingerie.

The blade had become a vessel for anger as my blood-soaked grip on the handle became tighter.

Seconds elapsed. It may have been minutes, but my legs somehow led me to the door. I pressed my hands against my ears as the undertones of James' sinful breath wailed through my mind. My destiny in life was to be alone.

Ajar became obtuse. Anger turned to pain. My darkest nightmare was now my reality.

James never spoke. He didn't need to. The bastard was too busy fucking a whore in my bed to say anything. I repeatedly banged my head against the door, yet it made no noise. I couldn't take my eyes away from him.

Once more, I was a woman scorned.

Hours ago, the sun shone brightly, and those birds whistled merrily in the nearby trees. I was all but a golden touch from the happiness I deserved. But joy and excitement became a twisted cradle of sorrow and desolation.

As the clock struck four, the knife fell silently to the rug. Why did it chime at three when it constantly dinged at five? Today was no different.

My body was gripped by an unstoppable force of skin-pinching detachment. I had to shake it off. I had to end the madness. I had to control the rage that went far beyond what lay beneath the rosebush.

There was no control, and my legs pushed me forward.

They were on my bed, both going at it like a needle to the vein. Why didn't he do those things to me? It was my fault. I shouldn't have pushed him into giving me what I once thought was possible. I shouldn't have pushed him into giving me something I desperately needed. He was to blame. James was a good-for-nothing sonofabitch.

Careful, Mommy. I don't like it.

I wanted to slug them where they fucked. I couldn't. I was too frozen to do anything but watch. Solitude was my friend. It was my isolated enemy.

James lay there with his hands behind his head as a blonde sucked on his nutsack. Had she ever been fed? I hated her. I hated her ass that was fatter than thunder. I hated the blue butterfly inked to her buttock.

A blue butterfly? How interesting.

I stepped into the bedroom and pointed the barrel toward them. "How could you do this to me, James?" I asked, unsure if I could handle the answer. "Why did you choose to destroy me?"

"Steph, what the fuck?"

"Hear me now, asshole! I won't hear excuses. You can save those for somebody who gives a damn. You're the reincarnation of that bastard in the garden. The rebirth of a slimy fuck. Ricardo broke my body, but you've shattered my mind. Why, James, why?"

He pushed Amanda away from his groin. She fell off the bed and down to the floor. "What the fuck?" she moaned.

"Steph, please let me—what happened to you?" James said, covering his groin. "You're splattered with blood."

I wiped the tears with a sleeve as my finger hovered closer to the deathpin. "You got your wish," I told him. "You have me destroyed, and this was a conspiracy. You conspired with Ricardo to drive me insane. It won't work. I'll never be crazy."

"You have this—"

"Don't speak, James," I warned. "Don't dare say another goddamn word! I refuse to listen to no rhyme or reason, and I'll hit the trigger if you open your mouth."

"Hear him out!" Amanda yelled, covering her droopy breasts with the bed sheet.

"Shut up, blondie! You're killing my concentration. That's right. I'm already digging your grave in my mind. Say another word, and that flutterbutter becomes toast a little earlier than I anticipated. It ends today. It ends for all of us."

Why touch cotton when silk runs through your soul?

CHAPTER SEVEN

James looked mortified as he continued to cover the guilt with his hands. "You don't have to do this, Steph. It ain't how it's supposed to—"

"You're a cheat. I hate you. Won't you shut your goddamn mouth already? It wasn't difficult to figure you out. Do you remember the conversation we had this morning? Do you recall asking when I'd return home? You had nowhere else to go. You couldn't wait until my back was turned before—"

"But you have this all—"

"Did I tell you to speak?" I pushed the barrel against his cheek before returning to the closet. "I expected this kind of thing from others, but not you. You were different. You said I was yours and how you could never love another. You begged to be part of my life, and I accepted. I gave you my trust. I'd have done anything for you, James."

My head rested against the doorframe as I smiled toward Amanda. All she did was stare at the ceiling, nodding her head.

"James, give her a nudge. She should witness what she's done to—look at the state of her. She'll need two coffins. One for each thigh, and her ass is a wow to humanity. She's a walrus carrying triplets. What did she give that was so damn special? What does she have that I don't? It's inexcusable. Denial is as bad as your actions."

My smile turned to fury.

I fired a shot to the right of his face, and there was now a hole in the wall no smaller than a baseball. This gun was more powerful than I thought, and the numbness in my shoulder was replaced by pain.

"Let it be a warning," I told them. "Anyway, it's time the whore earned her corn. Take off a sock. Do it now! Take off a sock and stick it in his mouth. It's one of those things you wear to cover your fat, hairy toes. Don't dare defy me. Oh, and keep your mouth closed. Save those excuses for your maker."

James was as white as the bed sheet when staring across the room at the tramp. He did nothing but muffle.

"Keep pushing my button, bastard. Not another goddamn word!"

This feels wrong, Mommy. I don't wanna play this anymore.

Amanda stared down the barrel of retribution. "Do you like my boyfriend's dick?" I said, pointing towards his groin. "Answer the freaking question, whore. Do you like his dick? Be clear with your reply. It may be the last time you ever speak."

She sobbed as her blood-red fingernails almost pierced the bed sheet. "Yes… I mean, no! Please don't hurt me. I'm… you don't have to do this."

There was so much satisfaction within me as I listened to her plead for her life. My finger became a little more twitchy.

"I'm confused," I said, smacking my forehead. "You don't like it but having it inside feels so good. Am I right? Is that what you're telling me? Any more bullcrap and you'll lose the face. Do you like his dick?"

"Yes!"

"Then suck it. Be quick. I've got Christmas to prepare. Did I pick up that turkey?"

Silence encompassed me. Just fleetingly.

"Somebody appears to have a problem with their hearing as well as their infidelity," I continued. "It's the Last Chance Saloon, blondie. Suck it, or mamma pulls the trigger!"

James tried to speak as his gaze desperately begged for forgiveness. His face reddened, and the veins in his neck pushed against his sweat-soaked skin.

And then she did it. Amanda tentatively reached for his dick. She couldn't look him in the eye. She did nothing but stare at his atom in a snowstorm.

"What are you waiting for, clown?" The rifle nodded and was ready for action. "Comply or die, Amanda. Work those lips. Use them or lose them. See how nice I am? You don't deserve options, but here I am, giving you them."

Her hand continued to tremble as she wrapped her dainty fingers around his lifeless embarrassment.

"What do I have to do to earn respect around here?" I asked, squeezing her jaw. She looked like a bloated fish. "Nobody listens. Amanda, I like you, but you're reluctant to do what I ask. Here's the deal. You suck, and I release the pressure off the trigger. There we go. It's easy. Faster, whore. Don't distract me. I need to know who to send to their grave."

He closed his eyes to the moment's thrill, his flaccidity immediately finding the life it once had. I hated that smile. I'd seen it hundreds of times whenever we made love.

Such tenderness could never be experienced again, not with me, James, or anybody. The game was almost finished.

CHAPTER EIGHT

The thought alone ripped through what remained of my broken mind, as the darkness grew blacker than ever. "Bite it off! You heard me, Ms. Flutterbutter. Bite off his goddamn dick!"

Mascara streamed down her pathetic, regretful face. Amanda was pretty. She would be to a shaggy mammoth, but she was now a cheap clown performing in a cheaper circus.

"Am I talking in a language you don't understand?" I asked, smacking the barrel twice against the top of her head. "I told you to bite off his dick. I'm just getting started."

His eyes remained closed, and he appeared to be getting off on it. He mustn't have heard my request.

"Would this be the third strike or a fourth?" I asked. "I've lost count, but you won't get another. Who would want to screw a woman who has no face? Nobody will kiss the lips you no longer have. I said now!"

Blood squirted in every direction as his limpness fell to the floor. James looked frantic when muffling loudly in pain. His hands were too busy gripping his meat to think about removing the gag. Perhaps it eased the pain.

There was something else that was extremely strange. I never recalled Ricardo having red tadpoles. His swimmers were a cowardly blend of yellow.

"Why do men make such a mess?" I asked, staring down at the shine of the knife. "First Ricardo, now you. Does anybody detect a theme here? Where was I? Oh, yes. You did it. It wasn't so hard… was it? Okay, maybe it was, but only after persuasion. Here comes the fun part. Put it in your mouth and swallow. Do it, or Momma goes bang."

As she tried to pick it up, James wailed like a baby. *Like the baby, I could never have.*

After numerous failed attempts, Amanda eventually got there. She appeared to be caught at a crossroads as blood dribbled down her chin. "Please don't… please, Steph. Please don't make me swallow it."

I'd never seen anybody shake so much, nor had I seen someone look so lost. "Swallow it, blondie. Swallow the lot!" I fired a second shot, and a clutch of splinters sliced into my hands. "Why am I repeating myself? It's as if some have lost their basic understanding of English. Do it, or I'll remove your face! I should have been a marine. It's a whole lot of fun."

Ms. Flutterbutter puddled in the slutty blue panties she no longer wore.

The guy of my dreams was now a haunting vision of my darkest nightmares.

Amanda began to choke. Death by dick. A punishment befitting of a two-dime whore.

James pushed the sock out of his mouth. "Please, Steph. You have it—you can't do this! I'm begging you to stop."

"Shut up. Shut up. Shut up! You wanted to take those swimmers to a different pool, so you pay the goddamn price. I guess yours have taken an early retirement."

"Let me help her! I need help, Steph. Let me call the…"

His body jolted as I hit the deathpin for a third time. Was it a fourth? It didn't matter. I was getting the hang of it. Dare I say it was fun?

Her face was a darker shade of purple as she tried to clear the obstruction. Those attempts were destined for failure.

"Did I bring in the groceries?" I asked. "Anybody?"

My finger was no longer itchy. It was now glued to the trigger, and a fourth shot ripped through the air.

It was the most powerful of them all, and I could no longer make out the color of her eyes. I could no longer smile at those tears. She possessed neither. There was more blood than Ricardo ever gave me, but Amanda's was blacker than sin.

James vomited where he struggled, and he fell to his side. His face was dripping in last night's dinner. "Steph… Steph… Steph, what have you done?" Tears gushed down his cheeks.

"Don't call me Steph! You never call me that. Ooh, listen up. I have a song. There once was a woman all covered in red. She fucked in my bed, then screwed with my head. I swore to take vengeance, so twisted and torn. You made that poor lady wish she'd never been born!"

I stared at the smoking barrel and smiled. "Did you see that brain? I didn't either. It's sludge. If I live to tell the tale, I should add color to the room. It won't be red. It's much too green for my liking."

I'd fallen into a chasm of anguish, yet there was no return. It was this morning when James said hello. It was hours later when he'd say goodnight.

"It's time we parted, but you did what Ricardo couldn't. You broke my mind. Well done. May your soul suffer in eternal damnation!"

Another shot cracked through the air.

CHAPTER NINE

James was still breathing, and this wasn't part of the deal. "Won't you die already?" I screamed in frustration.

A further three shots found a home deep in his chest.

Mommy, what have you done?

"Not now, Oscar. It's not the best time to have this conversation. No more lies, James. No infidelity. No excuses. You were my dream, but now it's over. You pushed me too far."

The gun fell, and I reached for the knife before perching on the floor.

Inch by inch, the blade disappeared deep into my womb. Claret dripped to the floor, and I became dizzy at the thought of living.

I looked at my dress, and what was once an innocent shade of white had become a deadly hue of red. There was no pain. There was nothing at all, and my womb destroyed me the day I was born.

My grip tightened. Black on black. Red to red. "If my child can't have it, then nobody will."

The blade went deeper, deeper, and deeper. I was the ultimate failure.

The rest of the steel disappeared, and a drip became a rampaging river. A riptide of heartless emotion.

But I stopped to the deafening footsteps beyond the door. It was the cops. It had to be. They were too late. The damage was much too terminal.

My contemptuous gaze met a vision of distortion, and my entire body shuddered as trauma shifted to a whole new level. It was a feral trick of the mind. It had to be. A blurred hallucination. How was this possible? "James?"

He threw the knife into the room's far corner. "Stephanie, what have you done?"

"It can't be. You're dead. I killed you. You were lying by the… you still are. What's happening to me, James?"

He fumbled for his cell phone. "I need medics! Send me the goddamn medics!"

The room fell upon a moment's silence.

"Yeah, it's Frampton Lodge near—be quick. I think they're dead. It'll be a third unless you get here quickly. Send me some freaking medics. Stephanie, no! Don't you dare close your eyes."

"James?" I called out his name, yet my lips never moved.

He slapped me repeatedly, but I was almost too numb to feel anything. "Stay awake, Stephanie!" he shouted, pushing open my eyes with his thumbs. "Hang in there for me, baby."

Why were there two of him? It didn't matter. I needed to sleep.

What I wouldn't give to see those beautiful blue trees in the swamp, the green sky, and that golden cloud. I'd been offered light yet fully grasped the encompassing darkness.

James wrapped me in his jacket as Chase burst into the room. I think it was him. "What happened?" he said, unable to look at Amanda for more than a second. "Medics? Get me those medics!"

Two were quick to join us. "We have a couple deceased," one said, "but the third's alive. Her pulse is—I want a bed. Get me a damn bed!"

"Please let me die," I whispered, my eyes feeling heavier than ever. "I need to sleep."

"Stay with me, lady. Nobody drifts on Paco's watch. Where's that bed?"

Chase led James away from the door. "What took place?" he asked, his eyes heavy and wide. "I want answers. I want them yesterday!"

"I don't know, Vic. I wasn't here. I called it—tell me this is a nightmare."

"You know them?"

"Will Stephanie be okay?" James threw back in panic.

"Answer me, Trapp! Do you know the deceased?"

James briefly paused to think about the question. "It's Amanda Heretic. She's the, umm, the owner of Heretic Hotdogs. It's my old boss. I'm struggling to breathe, but it's her. I can tell by the tattoo."

"And the guy?"

"Do I need to answer that question? It's my twin brother, Bobby Trapp. Could it not be more obvious?"

You could say there are one or two similarities.

"Help me, James. Please help me. I'm... I didn't know."

"I'm here, Stephanie. I'm not leaving your side."

My lids conceded to the darkness—I'm sure they did, as my surroundings were different when I opened them again. A click of a pen, the quiet prayer, two frantic calls for security.

Everything seemed to echo at least three times before drifting to a veil of nothingness.

I was trapped amid a hollow from hell. It was deeper than hell. I tried to climb out, but the flames were far too hot. I screamed. I tried, yet there was nothing there. I was finally defeated.

James squeezed my hand as they rushed me through a set of green doors. I think they were doors, and I'm sure they were green. I didn't know anymore.

"Can you save her?" he asked, his voice booming off the walls.

"Who is this guy?" the doctor said. "Get him out of here and let me do my goddamn job!"

"It doesn't answer the question! Can Stephanie be saved?"

"She's hemorrhaging by the—it's touch and go," the doctor replied. "Her chance will increase if you get out the damn way. Denise, tell them we're coming through. Run! We could lose her any minute."

"Can she pull through?"

The doctor pushed James away from the gurney. "She's in God's hands. We need a miracle, but she's lost the baby. Now, get out of my way. There's a life to save."

Silence never sounded so loud. It wasn't possible. It had to be a lie, a mistake, or anything else except the truth.

"I'm not following," said James. "You're telling me she was carrying?"

"I'd say about—let's move it along, people! Prepare yourselves for a very long night. Could somebody get this guy out of my face?"

I wanted to scream, but my throat had abandoned me. I

was powerless to do anything as my wrists were chained to the gurney. What had I done wrong?

I had to stay awake. I needed answers to questions yet to be asked. Weak became strengthless when a jab was delivered to my arm.

My lids succumbed to the inevitable.

CHAPTER TEN

December 25, 2018

I woke to the annoying sound of footsteps. Two distorted figures stood at the base of my bed, but I knew who they were. I remained chained to the rail.

"But I don't understand?" James said, his arms folded. "Stephanie had an appointment at Sixfields and wouldn't have missed it for the world. No, I don't buy it. I call bullshit!"

"About that appointment," Chase replied, flipping the lid of his laptop. "We captured everything on film, so you may wanna look at the footage. I'll warn you now. It ain't pretty. I just gotta figure out how to use it."

"Hitting play usually works," James sarcastically replied.

The room fleetingly fell to a hush, but then came the sporadic sound of passing cars.

"Okay, I got there," Chase eventually said. "You see the car in the lot? Even a blind man can see Ms. Black banging on that dash. Check out the time."

"Nine fifty-four. I don't understand?" James wasn't the only one confused. I didn't recall doing such a thing.

"What time was her appointment?" Chase returned.

"But why hasn't she left the car? Something's drastically wrong."

"Let's roll it to ten-oh-three a.m. Give it a few seconds.

You'll see those clinic doors come into the shot. Tell me who comes out of those doors."

There was again a period of silence.

"A guy in a suit," James said, shoulders hunched. "It means nothing to me, so won't you quit talking in riddles?"

"Dr. Forlorn was going for coffee as his previous appointment hadn't turned in. Ms. Black was that previous appointment. If only he realized what was coming his way. Okay, it's back to scoping the car. The door's open, but where is she? Give it time. The question will soon be answered."

The last thing I remembered was switching off the TV in the cabin. It was frustrating. The pill wouldn't have been so bitter if I recalled those missing memories.

"See what she's holding?" Chase said, pointing at the screen. "It's a blade. Turn away if you're squeamish."

"What's she doing? No, turn it off! Turn off the recording! Was that real?"

"She stabs him seven times in total. Two nurses try to help but don't make it past that—"

"But she sliced their throats!" James sounded traumatized. "Why are you showing me this? Wait, she's covered in blood. It's like she doesn't even know it."

"There was a third girl. She worked the desk, but she got lucky. The lady returned inside and locked the doors. She was one of many who called it through. Look at this. Look at Ms. Black's face as she drops the blade to the lawn and moves back to the Audi. No emotion. That's a blank stare if ever I saw one. Poor thing. You're witnessing her mind snapping. She never deserved it."

James fell silent as if to question the footage in front of him. He swiftly moved to the window but then returned to my bedside. My eyes were now firmly closed.

"It's not Stephanie," he said. "They're not the actions of the woman I know."

"You ain't known her," Chase replied. I felt his laptop brush against my leg. "Except for a shrink called Dr. Butcher, nobody ever has. I was digging, and you ain't never gonna believe what she's been through. Let's talk about her pregnancy. You realize it's the third time she's held a little one, right?"

"You're wrong, it's twice."

"I spoke to Dr. Butcher. He hid behind some confidentiality bullshit, but I got answers. I always do. It was years ago when Ms. Black was one of his patients. He tells me that what we saw were the last two pregnancies. You ain't got any idea about the first. The kid was thirteen years young. Let it sink in. Thirteen years young. Guess who the father would've been?"

James squeezed my hand. "I've only known her a year."

"The name Gerrard Black ring any bells?" Chase asked.

"Her father?"

"Only he wasn't her father. Not biologically. That was her stepfather. Her original name is Stephanie Winters. Name only changed through her mother's marriage, but nobody made the connection. He sexually abused her for years, and it was little wonder why she snapped. It would've been tough to prosecute. How do you find evidence if it no longer exists? I'd loved to have nailed that sonofabitch to the wall."

"Why are you talking in past tense?"

"Let me finish, Trapp," Chase said. "No matter how tough she had it, the poor girl wouldn't abort. Guess she ain't a believer in termination. That pregnancy almost went the distance, but her heart must have broken when she delivered a stillborn. It was something like that."

James rose to his feet and began pacing the room. "I could kill him for what he—"

"Ms. Black left the parking lot at ten fourteen, but it was a short while later when dispatch took a call. A gray Silverado was seen hitting speeds higher than a hundred. We thought it was—"

"She no longer has a Silverado. Stephanie sold it months ago."

I momentarily opened my eyes to see Chase nodding. "We followed to Henderson, but it wasn't Ms. Black. Her mom, Jacqueline, lived close by, so my men paid her a visit."

"Let me get this straight," James shot back, his hands resting on his elbows. "You were sharing cookies with her mom while my brother was being dragged through hell? Is that how it happened? Oh, wow, Jacqueline doesn't know. She'd be here if she did. I need to call her. She needs to know what's happened to her daughter."

"There was nobody home," Chase added. "My men snooped behind the cabin but were beaten back by decomposition. It came from an outhouse at the back of the garden."

"Jacqueline's dead?"

I felt excess weight at the foot of my bed. "Two corpses, both headless," said Chase.

"No, she wouldn't have—Stephanie thought the world of her mom."

"We found the heads minutes later. They were inside the stove and cooking on a very low heat. I ain't saying Ms. Black's responsible, but it sure looks that way. It happened yesterday. I believe she called time on her predator. I also think her mom was the silent witness who should've offered her girl some protection. We'll know more after speaking to Ms. Black."

I think she's spending the entire day cooking for Pops.

The door opened, and in came more footsteps. "Mr. Trapp, you asked a question last night, but I didn't have the answers."

It was the very doctor who took me into surgery. "We've run some tests, but the news isn't good. Ms. Black will never conceive. There's been too much damage done to her uterus and the surrounding area. Her self-inflicted cuts were extensive."

"But it makes no sense," James returned. "Why didn't she enter the clinic?"

"We'll do a full evaluation, but based on what I've witnessed, I believe the fear of failure was the cause. I've seen it before. The mind goes into defensive mode. It snaps as it processes the rejection. She won't be the first, nor will she be the last to suffer such trauma. It's my opinion, nothing more. Don't quote me on that. Go home and rest. You'll need—"

"Ain't a good idea," Chase added. "He needs to spend time with his lady. Ms. Black's down for a stainless-steel ride if the DA gets his way. She ain't never gonna see the light of day, regardless. Just saying how it is."

I did attend the appointment. I'm sure I did, but I couldn't remember.

Reality funneled me into a one-way tunnel of skin-pinching darkness. I'd killed my heart's desire. I'd destroyed everything I'd ever dreamed of. It was time to check out.

My left arm tingled as the unmistakable stench of a swamp filled the air. Then came the pain in my chest.

"She's flatlined!" the doctor shouted. "Nurses, get in here now!"

"No, Stephanie! Please don't do this to me. Come back to me, baby. Stay with me!"

I embraced that darkness.

THE END

Printed in Great Britain
by Amazon